GRAHAM

EMERSON WOLVES BOOK 6

KATHI S. BARTON

This is a work of fiction. Names, characters, places, and incidents are products of the author's imagination or are used fictitiously and are not to be construed as real. Any resemblance to actual events, locations, organizations, or persons, living or dead, is entirely coincidental.

World Castle Publishing, LLC
Pensacola, Florida
Copyright © Kathi S. Barton 2016
Paperback ISBN: 9781629896076
eBook ISBN: 9781629896083
First Edition World Castle Publishing, LLC, December 12, 2016
http://www.worldcastlepublishing.com

Licensing Notes

Cover: Karen Fuller
Editor: Maxine Bringenberg

PROLOGUE

"I tell you, Ram, that daughter of yours is a hoot. I just asked her what she thought of all this, and she said that the money from what was going to be tossed out when this was over could have fed an entire village for a week."

Ram Stockholm looked around the room for his daughter. "When did you speak to her? I thought her and Chad had left for their honeymoon already." There was no way his daughter would say that about her own wedding. At least he hoped not. But she was a little stressed out right now. Christ, they'd spent a fortune on this thing, and to have her upset wasn't going to happen. Not that his baby girl didn't deserve it, but to say something like this to William Frank was terrible.

"No, no. I meant Ramsey. To tell you the truth, Ram, I had no idea you had another child, much less one as beautiful as she is. But she's the spitting image of you now that I think on it." Ram wondered about Ramsey, his youngest child, as William continued. "Like I said, a beautiful little thing, but a mite outspoken. I'd wondered why you didn't have her up there with her sister, but I'm assuming that the two of them don't get along."

"They don't. Where did you see her go? I'd like to speak to her." William laughed and pointed to the large open doors at the back of the large room. "Excuse me."

If William answered him, he didn't hear him. Ramsey wasn't going to ruin her sisters' day by complaining about something that was none of her business. But as soon as he stepped out on the deck to talk to her, he stilled. When the hell had she grown up?

The dark blue dress she had on made the paleness of her porcelain skin almost glow. With her hair done up in one of those complicated twists, it gave her neck a gracefulness that would make most men he knew drool. She was tall too, Ram just realized, and rail thin. He cleared his throat before going out all the way. When Ramsey turned his way, Ram thought that he'd made a mistake…this could not be his child.

"Hello, Dad."

Ram moved out to stand beside her. He was speechless. Not only was this his child, but she'd grown up before…well, she had.

"I just talked to William. He said you were a hoot." Ramsey looked at him, confused. "William Frank. His son is going to Yale right now. I guess you told him we spent too much on this wedding. Why would you say something like that?"

"I didn't. Well, I did, but not like that. He asked me if I was going to have an extravagant wedding like this in a few years, and I told him no. If I ever get married, I want it simple, and the money spent on all this could go to some charity to feed the hungry. There are quite a few of them right here in our own town." She looked at him as she continued. "Deidra is pissed at me again."

"Don't talk like that. You're not old enough to use that kind of language." She laughed, a harsh sound that seemed to him like she too was upset. "What did you do to her this time, Ramsey?"

As soon as the words left his mouth, he knew that he'd made a mistake. But the two of them, along with Gregory, their brother, had been fighting since the day that Ramsey was brought home from the hospital, or so it seemed. He just wanted peace and quiet. He never got it when they were all together. And now that he thought about it, he'd not seen them all together in a good long time. Ramsey had been… well, he had no idea where she'd been of late.

"First of all, I'm nineteen. Secondly, I didn't do anything other than to show up here. She seems to think that I'm going to embarrass her because I'm not in the wedding party. And people—her kind, she called them—would ask questions." Ram started to ask her why she wasn't in the party, but Ramsey spoke again. "She didn't ask me to be in it, if you were going to ask me. And when I asked her about it, she told me that I would never fit in. Deidra said that she wanted people in her party that were nice and beautiful, something that I'm certainly not."

"I'll talk to her." He would too. He thought this feuding had gone on long enough. "To be honest with you, Ramsey, I almost didn't know who you were when I came out here. And where have you been hiding yourself? You look lovely."

"Thanks."

He nodded, then followed her when she moved to sit in one of the chairs that had been brought for people to use. The country club where Deidra's wedding reception was being held was very accommodating. But he supposed that had to do with his money rather than who he might be. They sat there for several moments before Ramsey spoke again.

"I'm leaving, Dad." He offered to get her a car to take her home. He asked her to tell the butler that they'd be along shortly. When she looked at him with the oddest look on her face, he wondered what he'd said wrong now. He was still trying to get over the fact that she was really nineteen. "I don't live at home, and I wasn't planning on going there anyway. I haven't lived there for some time now. Dad, do you know anything about me? What I do for a living? Where I live?"

He was embarrassed that he didn't know the answer to any of those things. And the worst part of it was, William wasn't the first person to ask him about Ramsey, saying that they had no idea he had a third child. *What have I done?* he asked himself. *And where the hell had all the time gone?*

Gregory was the oldest, and had gotten into college on a sports scholarship. He'd been struggling in high school, so it had come as a surprise to know that a college was willing to take him. Gregory had always been more of a player than a scholar. Now he was living at home again, with nothing to show for his six years at a very expensive and prestigious university.

Deidra had been, like her mother before her, the prom queen every year since she'd gotten to junior high. Before that she'd been in countless pageants, and had won most of those as well. She was pretty, and vain enough to make them work for her. Now at twenty five she was newly married to a man that Ram didn't like, and hated to have around for any reason.

But his baby had wanted him, and he'd done everything in his power to make sure she had what she wanted...or, he supposed, what his wife had wanted for her. He'd been involved in their lives. From the time they were old enough to enter things, sometimes even before that, he and his wife Krista had been there for them. But not Ramsey. He couldn't remember a single moment, sports event, or even a play that he'd gone to for his youngest child.

"I've never...I'm sorry to say, I don't know any of those things." He looked away from her knowing face and continued. "I can't remember one single play that we attended that you were in. Not a game of any sort that you might have been in. Nor do I remember having any sort of graduation party when you got out of school last year." He looked at her then. "I'm drawing a blank as to what I got you for your sixteenth birthday. What I got you for your eighteenth or any in-between, and I haven't the slightest idea what you've been up to since you got out of school."

"I graduated from high school six years ago. So no, you didn't have a party for me. I think that Deidra said it would mess up her summer plans with her friends or something like that. I just finished up my last year of college last month, and I'm nearly done with my master's degree as well. I moved out when Mom told me to because I was bothering Deidra too much and it was getting on her nerves. That would have been right after I turned seventeen and was nearly finished with college. I work for...." She stood up and he did as well. "It doesn't matter now. But I'm going away. And...I have a job opportunity and I'm going to take it."

"Going away to where? And what are you going to do for

this company?" Her laugh hurt him. "Ramsey, I'm so sorry. I wish I could tell you that I do remember all of this, but I don't want to lie to you. I feel like this is all my fault. Don't leave. Please. I'd like for you to move back home and for us to get to know one another. It's not too late, is it?"

"You mean because Deidra is gone now, you wouldn't mind me being there?" Ram felt as if she'd stabbed him in the heart. But if she thought that she'd hurt him, he couldn't see it on her face. And it was nothing less than he deserved. "No thanks. I think…I think that after all this time, it would just be an embarrassment for all of us."

"Ramsey, let me make this up to you. Please don't go like this. I've messed up badly, but this is…we're family, after all." She only stood there with her back to him. Ram wanted to take her into his arms and hold her, but he didn't know how. In all honesty, he didn't remember a single time when he'd hugged his baby. "Will you at least call me sometimes? Weekly?"

"I don't know. I'll try." She turned then and looked at him. "My plane leaves at six in the morning. I've taken care of my house and all my bills, so there is no reason for you to be bothered by that. And I've sold off all the things that I no longer need. So…well, I guess this is goodbye for a while."

As she walked away and out of his life, all Ram could think about was that he'd wasted a lot of his life and hers not getting to know her. It both saddened him and made him hate himself that he'd done this to her. Not just him, but all of them had. Sitting down on the chair again, he thought of all the times he and his wife would talk about Deidra and Gregory. What they were doing. How they were doing in school. Conversations about Ramsey were few and far between. And worse yet, when they did speak of her, mostly his wife, it was about how she was nothing like them and how she'd never fit in properly with them. That if she were more like her brother and sister, perhaps they'd take her to more places. Ram would never forgive himself.

~~~

Ramsey drove home wondering if she'd done the right thing. Her original plan had been to simply leave without telling them, but then her dad had come out to talk to her and she'd told him. It wouldn't be like them to miss her or anything. In fact, she was pretty sure that not one of them would have given her a second thought. But her dad had hurt her, and she thought that she wanted to hurt him back for a change. Well, she was sure she had, and herself as well. Going into her little house, she thought of the cases that she'd packed over the last week. She had no idea if she'd be back here again, but really couldn't see any reason to return. So what she didn't put into storage—and she'd stored very little—had been given away, sold, or just donated to whoever had wanted it. Which again, wasn't all that much.

She'd sold her house the week before, and had thirty days to leave before the new owners would be taking it. Ramsey had already sold most of her furniture, and all she had left was the bed that she'd been sleeping in and a single dresser. There were no mementos in the house that she was taking. No pictures of her family because she didn't have any, and there were no pets in her life. Ramsey had made such a tiny footprint in her life so far, and she was looking forward to making more.

Putting all her cameras away except the one that she'd

taken to Deidra's wedding, she made her way to the darkroom. Her plane didn't leave until late tomorrow night, but she'd told her dad differently because she didn't want him to think they could get together beforehand. Ramsey had meant nothing to them before this, and she saw no reason to try and cram a lifetime of conversations and hugs into her last day. Neither of them would be very comfortable with that, and she was pretty sure it would piss off her mother. The woman had never really liked her, not even as a child. Ramsey had long since given up on trying to do something that would get her noticed, and had gone on with her life as if they'd never been a part of it.

The pictures that she'd taken at her sister's wedding were all on a clip, and she ran them through the computer to see which ones she wanted to print. While it downloaded them onto the hard-drive, she went to change into more comfy clothes. Ramsey had no idea if her sister would ever see the pictures that she'd taken, or even if she'd want them. Sending them to her father, she decided suddenly, was the best way to get them to her, and she hoped that he'd at least look. The camera, or what she could do with it, was her passion.

Just as she was hanging the last of the prints up to dry, Ramsey heard her phone ringing. Turning on the lights overhead, she made her way to it as she dried her hands. She knew who it was before she picked it up, and decided that as soon as possible she was going to change her number. This guy was a pain in the ass. And if he'd known who she was and who he worked for, he'd back the fuck off.

"I just heard that you're leaving. When did this take place? I'd very much like to have you come in before you leave, Miss

Holms. The job that I have for you is still open." Ramsey looked through the mail as he continued talking, wondering if the change of her name when she worked was enough to distance her from her family. "I have a noon opening, and also one at two. Which one can I put you down for?"

"Neither." He laughed a little on the other end. Ramsey put the mail, mostly credit card applications, in the trash and pulled a paper bowl from the sleeve to have some cereal. "I really have to go, Mr. Carter. I have things to do."

"Wait. This is the job of a lifetime, Miss...can I call you Ramsey? This is the job of a lifetime. This is a large paper and very prestigious. Think of what doors it could open for you in the long-term." She didn't answer him but yawned. "Ramsey, tell me what I need to do to have you come here and work for us."

"There is nothing you can do. I do not want to work for you. I have a job, one that I wanted and worked hard for. I'm sorry, but you'll have to find someone else." She hung up as he was speaking. Then when she was sure that he wasn't going to be on the other end, she put a block on his number and sent it directly to her voicemail. He'd more than likely still call and fill up the message box, but for now she was happy.

The stupid man worked for her father, as he owned the paper that Mr. Carter thought she should come to work for. And not only that, but the job that he wanted her to take? She'd been doing it all the way through college to make ends meet. It had always surprised her that not once in all that time had she ever run across her family.

After making sure that everything was turned off in the darkroom, she made her way to her room after eating the last of her cereal. The bed wasn't made, of course, but she didn't care. Taking the last of her suitcases off it, Ramsey stripped down and laid out on the messy bed. She was asleep almost immediately.

Two hours later she was awake and refreshed. Taking a long hot shower, Ramsey thought of where she might be going. And when she got there, what she was going to do first.

Ramsey didn't have a job to go to like everyone thought. She'd said that to her dad to make sure he didn't worry. Moot point, she supposed, since he'd not cared before. But she was going somewhere. Ramsey didn't even have a destination in mind, not really, but she was going to South Africa. And she was going to take pictures of everything. And a lot of them.

By six that night she had everything printed and the pictures—which she'd made extras of for her dad—in a box. Affixing a label to the box, she put it near her luggage so she'd remember to mail it. Sitting down on the floor in the kitchen, she tried to remember if she had everything she was going to need.

At seven she picked up the last of her things and was headed out the door and locking it up when someone came up behind her. Lucky for him, or maybe herself, she was able to stop herself from knocking her dad on his ass. Ramsey asked him what he was doing there.

"I'm a very resourceful man when I need to be, Ramsey. And I realized that if you left today, without me even talking to you once more, I wouldn't get to see you again. I think... well, you have no reason to want me in your life, but I would very much like for you to try and have me in it." He took the biggest suitcase from her and put it in his car. "I paid the driver that was here. I'll make sure you get to the airport on time."

"Why are you doing this? I thought we cleared things up last night." She was still standing on her stoop when he came back for the other piece of luggage. "Dad? What are you really doing here?"

"How about if we have dinner before you go? I know you have time. We can even eat in the airport if you want. I just... I'd like to have dinner with you before you go. I don't deserve this chance, and Lord knows that you have every reason to tell me to go to hell, but I need this, Ramsey." She asked him why again. "Because I need to connect with you, and will take whatever.... No, that's not quite right. I do want to be with you tonight, but I also wanted to make sure you knew how serious I was about you calling me. I thought...I hoped that I could convince you that I love you."

"I love you too, but this is unnecessary. Besides, I was just going to grab a burger at the airport, then wait for my flight. Dad, what does Mom think about you being here?" When he looked away, she knew. "She told you not to come here, didn't she? It's all right, Dad. Whatever she said, I'm sure she was right."

"She said you were trying for attention. You weren't going anywhere, but acting out because you weren't the center of attention at the wedding. I told her she couldn't have been more wrong. You've never wanted to be there before. That's more Deidra's style, not yours." He took the box from her and noticed that it had his name on it. "What's this?"

"I took some pictures at the wedding and thought she'd want them. Or you might. I don't care. I don't even know why

I took them other than I wanted to do it. It was just…I don't understand any of this." He laughed, and it sounded so sad that she had to brace herself when the pain tore at her heart. "You should go back home before Mom gets upset."

"She already is. And it's doubtful that she's going to be in any better mood from now on." He shut the trunk of his car and turned to her. "Where are you going, Ramsey? Please let me know that much. Not that I deserve it, but I'd like to know."

"My first stop is in South Africa. The next…I don't know. I don't have a plan or a job. I just know that I can't be here and not be in your lives anymore." He nodded as if he already knew that. "Dad, it's all right. I've told myself that you had the other two, and Mom has often told me that I wasn't planned. It's fine."

"But it's not. It's not fine at all. Not for me. I screwed up. Now I want to…I don't know what I want, but I know that I want to get to know you. Start over, I guess."

Ramsey looked at the big moving van coming down the street. Going to her dad's car, she wasn't surprised that he opened the door for her. He was old world all the way to his little bow tie he always wore. When he got in on the driver's side, she told him she was ready and they drove off. Ramsey tried her best not to see the van pulling up in front of her little house so they could strip out the rest of her things. The darkroom would be picked up later that day by someone from the high school as a donation to their art department. And that would be it. Everything that she'd been would be gone in a matter of hours. It would be as if Ramsey Stockholm had never been.

The trip to the airport didn't take long. Her dad asked her questions and she answered them. Not anything too personal, she realized, but he was trying. When he parked, he took most of her luggage and she her carry-on things. He had the box of pictures under his arm, and when she asked him about that, he laughed.

"I want to see them while you're here so that I can tell you what a great job you did." He laughed again when she told him they might be crap. "Nah, I don't think so. I found out you're pretty famous with your camera. I mean, you are R. S. Holms, aren't you? I had no idea."

"No one does. And I'd like to keep it that way." He nodded as they made their way through the line to have her luggage checked. "Those pictures aren't your normal wedding kind of thing. Most of them are candid shots that I had fun taking. You really might think they're crap when you see them."

"I highly doubt that. You're quite famous as a photographer, aren't you? The article I read about you, they don't know who you are, do they? No one even knows that you're a female." She shook her head. "I'm glad I looked. I almost skipped over the article because it said you weren't who I was looking for. Why did you change it?"

"My personal life is just that. Personal. And if I put out there that I was who I am, I think any doors that would have opened for me when I started taking pictures would have been because of your last name. This is all mine, not the family's." She wondered if she might have hurt him again, but he smiled at her. "I wanted to do this on my own, and I did it."

"You certainly did, and I understand that." She wasn't sure he did but said nothing. "While our name means a great deal around the world, you just wanted to make it without my help. I'm proud of you for that."

"Thank you."

After her luggage was tagged and taken away, they decided to have dinner at one of the nicer restaurants in the place. Ramsey had about three hours before her plane took off, and she wasn't sure she wanted to sit with her dad while waiting. He seemed to genuinely want to be with her, but she was sure that he'd get bored after a while and want to cut it short.

When he ordered his dinner then she hers, he pulled out the box and opened it. The very first picture was of Deidra standing in her room with her sweat pants and tee shirt on, with her wedding gown hanging from the hook on the wall. He pulled it from the box and studied it.

"That dress alone could have fed an entire village." She laughed when he did. "I guess I'm odd when I think that the money could have been better spent. Like on a house or something. But I guess they have their own ideas of what is going to work in their own lives. What that is, I have no idea, but that's what she said to me. I don't care for Chad all that much anyway."

"To be honest with you, neither do I. And we did buy them a house, but...well, Chad, I found out, has a bit of a gambling problem, and I made him a deal. I'll use what I paid for the house to pay the debt off, and he'll be on his own." He shook his head. "I have a feeling that this is never going to be the end of it for them. And Gregory is...well, I don't want to talk about them right now."

He had made his way through about half the pictures

when their dinner came. Ramsey had the grilled salmon with grilled scallops on the side, plus a huge baked potato. Her dad, a steak and potatoes man, had ordered a beautiful porterhouse with the same potato with butter and sour cream. No salads for either of them.

When he looked at the last picture in the box, she felt herself getting uncomfortable. He stared at the last one for so long that she wanted to ask him what was wrong with it. Her dad looked at her with tears in his eyes and she felt her heart twist.

"The only family picture in the world that is half assed. You should have been in this with us. Obviously you were there. Why didn't you join us?" She just shook her head and he nodded as if he might know. "Was it your mom or Deidra that told you to step out of the picture? I have no doubt, after this, that it could have been both of them."

"I understand why she didn't want me there. It was Deidra's day, not mine." That wasn't really what was said to her, but it was less painfully said her way. "But the picture turned out nicely, didn't it?"

"It did. I believe that these pictures are going to be much nicer than the ones we paid that man too much money to take. But I want to know. What did your mother say to you, Ramsey? I need to know." She didn't want to tell him. But then she thought what the hell, I'm leaving and more than likely won't be back. "Ramsey?"

"She told me it was for the family and not for upstarts like me. I started to point out that I was her daughter too when she...she slapped me. Told me that she wished I'd not been born. I unbalanced her life. Unbalanced? How did I...? I had no say in being born. Why does she say things like that to me?" She turned away from him to finish. "To be honest with you, it was the deciding factor in my leaving without saying a word to any of you. I don't know why I even told...yes I do. I wanted to hurt you like you all have hurt me my entire life. That's the only reason that I even told you I was going."

"I don't know why she'd say those things to you. I really don't. But I am glad that you told me. It afforded me this, this opportunity to see if I could patch things up—even if it is nearly too late—between us." He pushed his plate away too. Her appetite was gone, as it appeared his was. "She said that I was a fool to try and mend the fences with you, even if that was what I was going to do. She blamed you for this and so many things that I don't even know how she thought you were a part of. I never realized the extent of her hatred for you. Saying that all you wanted was for...well, you know what she said. All the attention. Then when I told her I was going to talk to you, she had a fit and ended up in bed with one of her headaches. I didn't stay to listen to her anymore. Gregory said he'd keep an eye on her for me."

"She hates me, Dad." He didn't say anything, and for that she was grateful.

The rest of the meal was spent not mentioning the family. Ramsey thought that was about as depressing as it could get. When her flight was called, he walked her to the barriers and pulled her into his arms.

"I'm sorry. So very sorry, honey." She told him not to worry about it. "I will, and I still am. But I want you to take this. It's a credit card with just your name on it. You can... if you want to come home sometime or anything, just use it.

And I have a number there that I want you to use. It's…well, it's mine and mine alone. If you can't get me that way, then use the house phone. But I want you to call me. Weekly if you can."

"I don't need this, Dad." He pushed it back at her when she tried to give it back. "Dad, you don't have to do this for me to call you. I will."

"It's not why I'm doing it. I want you to have a backup plan. A way to come home to me if you need me." She wanted to tell him she needed him years ago, but said nothing. "I wasn't there for you for nineteen years, Ramsey, but I want to be now."

Nodding, she was moving to the gates when he called her back. This hug she returned, and felt better when they parted ways. Ramsey cried all the way to her first stop, and got off the plane with a heavy and saddened heart.

CHAPTER 1

Nine years and four months later

"We're set to open soon, and you have no idea where he is, do you?" Sloan wasn't in the best of moods, and this jerk in front of her was making her wolf want to tear him apart. And trying to talk to him in reasonable tones was giving her a headache. "You said that he'd be here last week. Now you're saying in three days. What the hell is going on? We have a contract with this man that you highly recommend, and so far I've not seen a whole lot of the professionalism you claim he has."

"Slo—" Sloan growled low in her throat. "Mrs. Emerson. Mr. Holms is coming, I assure you. And the only information I could get from his lawyer is that things are delayed. I asked him what was the problem, and he said it has been taken care of now and that R.S. was on his way."

"We have our grand opening very soon, Mr. Cocksure." She watched his face when he realized that she'd said his name wrong again. When he corrected her, for probably the fiftieth time, she continued. "Mr. Conrad, if he's not here by tomorrow morning, I don't want him here at all. Do I make myself perfectly clear? This gallery is going to open, and if he doesn't want to show, I'll have all his things put back into storage and have them returned to wherever this person is."

"Yes ma'am."

Sloan walked away feeling better for getting the man to shake up a little. She didn't like intimidating people, but she'd promised Clemmie and Kimber that she'd help. Well, she was helping them, all right. But the man who was their headliner and somewhat of a coordinator, so to speak, hadn't bothered calling her or her manager, and she was pissed.

As Sloan started out the door of the big mansion, she saw the woman coming toward her. Even before she was close enough to smell, Sloan knew she was hurt. Her entire body was stiff with profound pain, and she'd bet anything that she wasn't supposed to be up and around, but was too stubborn to heed anyone's advice. When she reached for the wall, to no doubt steady herself, Sloan hurried to her. But before she touched her, the woman flinched away from her.

"No offense, lady, but if you touch me somewhere that I'm hurt, I'm going to fucking lose it. If you could even find a place where I don't hurt I think I'd still cry out in pain." Sloan told her she should have a seat until she felt better. "I have an appointment with some jerk wad named Conrad. And if he's as nasty to me in person as he is in his emails, he might not make it to the end of the day. I was supposed to be here last week, but I had a slight problem."

"You're R. S. Holms?" The woman nodded as she moved to the set of chairs that had only just arrived today. "I thought you were a man…well, I think we all did."

"You were supposed to." As she sat, a bottle of water and

a medicine bottle were pulled from the pocket in her hoodie. "This Conrad guy…he here? I don't want you to tell me if he is. I have a picture of him in my mind and I want to pick him out."

"He's here." Sloan sat down across from her and watched as her already pale face seemed to grow whiter. "Should you be here? I mean, up and around?"

"Conrad is about five feet five inches or so. Really short hair, with a balding spot on the top of his head that he hopes no one will notice." Sloan looked over at Conrad and smiled. "He wears these really ugly suits, not because he wants to be stylish, but because he wants to stand out in a crowd. Not that he wouldn't anyway with that nasty limp he has. How am I doing?"

"Dead on except for the limp. He doesn't have one so far as I've seen." Ramsey looked at the man that Sloan had pointed to. "And the suits, why on earth would you know about that?"

"It's a game I play. I meet a lot of people in my job, and I like to sum up those that I don't." Ramsey leaned back on the seat again. "I'm sorry I'm late. But I had some problems and couldn't leave before today. Doctors can be such a pain in the fucking ass, can't they?"

"You were hurt, and badly if I don't miss my guess. So maybe they were right in this." Sloan liked the woman. She knew that she'd only just met her, but she really liked her. Sloan thought that her sisters would as well. "Should you even be up and around?"

"I'm wondering if when you open the doors you will have any kind of front and center people. A butler, or a guy dressed to look like one, would be nice, even if he's only there to direct people where they can hang their coats and jackets. In tails, if you can get them. Kind of old world that looks down his nose at people, but in a sort of nice way." Sloan pulled out her tablet and started making notes. "Kids...you need teenagers there, and take away their cell phones so they interact with real people rather than the ones on their phone. About ten should do it. I'm to understand that you have nine rooms or so, with different styles of art in each one? Have the kids dress accordingly. Modern art would have one dressed in something artsy. Kinda dark and brooding, I think. Paintings should have a kid that knows the difference between brushes and rollers dressed in something hip and fun. You get the idea."

"Yes. We hoped to have more artists, but there just weren't a lot of people willing to come and show off their works in such a small setting." She said she'd make some calls. "I guess you think this is beneath you."

"Why?" Sloan had no idea why she'd said that other than the fact that this woman was known worldwide for her work. "I'm just a person like you. I might know a few things about taking pictures, but I don't have any clue how to raise a garden and bring a business back to life when it's going to fail."

"You investigated me." Ramsey nodded but didn't say anything. "Then it should be no surprise that I had you looked into as well. But there is nothing out there about you. Not even what sex you are."

"And I like it that way." When she yawned again, Sloan asked her if she needed to lie down. "No thanks. But you will remember, Mrs. Emerson, that I'm here only as a consultant, for all you know. No one will know who I am or I will sue you, all right? I've agreed to have my work here to bring in some of the higher end buyers, but I don't want anyone to come and want me to take a selfie with them."

"What do we call you then? I'm sure that Ramsey is not a name that many have, and fewer of them women. But we can work around that as you go by your initials."

She nodded, but it was slower this time, almost as if she were nearly asleep. Her voice, when she did speak, was low and sort of slurred.

"Since they're looking for a man named R. S., then I'm pretty sure that I won't be recognized at all." When she stood up suddenly, Sloan felt her wolf move along her skin. Her smile made her think that she'd felt her too. "You're not human, are you?"

"No. Are you?" Ramsey nodded. "But you know what I am, so that means you've had some dealings with our kind."

"A little. Mind if I have a look around alone? I want to see what I can set up for you at the last minute."

Sloan told her to go ahead. As soon as she left her to take a tour, Sloan reached for Hunter.

She's here. R. S. Holms is here, and she's a she. She heard him laughing and wanted to smack him in the head. *Also, she's not all that open. I wish that Addie were here to see what is going on with her. I don't know what happened, but she's very hurt. Injured in some way she won't talk about.*

Shut you down, did she? She must be ballsy if she won't answer your questions. He was teasing her into a better mood, and it was working. *Why don't you come back here and I'll show you how sorry I am that she hurt you.*

27

You ever think of anything besides sex? He told her no, then asked if there was anything besides sex. *Yes, you moron, there are a great many things other than sex. I have to get going here. Ramsey is coming toward me, and she does not look well.*

"How...? Okay, let me think.... There is a room at the top of the stairs that had some...I guess it's a storage room, right?" Sloan nodded. "Great. Can we empty it out and use it? I have an artist that said she'll be able to get here in time, but she needs to have a room. I guess she had a show that was a bust, so she had some inventory. And I want to warn you now, she's beyond weird. Nice and very good, but weird all the same."

"I can handle weird, I think. The storage stuff can be moved to the back of the building where we didn't have it renovated yet. Let me call in some pack and get started." When Ramsey sat down, hard, Sloan went to her. "Where are you hurting? I think after this, I should get to know that much."

Instead of answering her, she lifted up her shirt. Sloan had always thought of herself as strong and nothing bothered her. But seeing the damage done to this woman made her belly lurch up. She'd been brutalized. And it looked like she'd been hurt recently too.

"I have no idea what you might have running through your head right now, but it looks serious. It isn't even close to what you're thinking." Sloan asked her if she could read her mind. "No. Can you? Never mind. It's not whatever you have going on in your head. I was hurt helping some kids out of a bad situation. It really didn't turn out well for them either, but I'm alive to walk away. Most of them, nearly all of them, didn't make it."

"When? How?" Ramsey only shook her head. "You're not going to tell me after showing me this? You need to tell me."

Sloan watched her face. The girl had blown off her compulsion like it was nothing. When Ramsey finally stood up, Sloan took a step back. There was something very strange about this one. For now, she wasn't afraid of her. But Sloan was frustrated by how vague she was about things. Mostly personal, but it was none the less frustrating.

"By pack, I'm assuming that you're a wolf?" Sloan nodded. "And if I don't miss my bet, you're also the alpha bitch."

"Yes. While I don't care for the word, that's what I am. My mate and husband is Hunter. Hunter Emerson. Have you heard of him?" Ramsey shook her head. "But you have heard of our kind. And have had dealings with them too, I'm betting."

"I have. The room? She's coming by tomorrow. I don't think she's expecting to be top billing, but you might want to make sure that she has a place to stay that's nice. I like her and all, but she's somewhat of a snob in addition to the weirdness." Sloan asked her who it was. "Margo Wainwright. Do you know her?"

"No, but I have heard of her. Margo...she wants to come here? To our gallery?" Ramsey said that she was. "Oh my. With the two of you here, we're going to have to do something—"

"I'm really sorry, but had I been on time, I might have gotten a few more to come in. As it is, Margo will be a good addition. Again, I'm really sorry for being late." Sloan nodded but watched her. "I don't want...you can have my things on display should you want them, but no one is to know who I am. We're okay with that, right? I like it that way. And no

29

pictures either. My work is fine, but not any of me."

"Are you on the run?" Ramsey said nothing but moved to the door. "I asked you a question, Ramsey. Will someone come here to harm you? Will my family be hurt?"

"No. No one will come to harm your family because I'm here. As for me hiding out, yes, in a way I am. But not in a nefarious way. Just...I guess you could say that I ran away from home, and I'm not ready to let them know that I'm back again." Sloan waited for more; she was sure there would be. "Just please do as I asked. No photos, and don't mention that Ramsey Holms is here. All right?"

"Yes."

She didn't look as if she believed her, but Ramsey finally left. When she was out the door, Sloan went to find the one person she knew could help her. Addie was just down the street at the diner, and she needed to talk to her.

~~~

Ramsey stared at the phone for ten minutes, willing it not to work. It would, there was no doubt about that. It was brand new and it had been charged for twelve hours. The only thing that could make it so that it never worked was for her not to ever touch it. No one but her had the number, and she wasn't going to share it any time too soon if she didn't just pick the fucker up and give the person she wanted to call the number. He wasn't going to be happy with her anyway, and right now, she wasn't too terribly happy with herself. But that was really nothing new.

She knew as surely as she was sitting there that things were going to go wrong in a heartbeat. As soon as she asked the alpha bitch not to take her picture or to mention she was here, it was going to go down badly. Not that anyone would be hurt. The only one that it could and would bother was her. But to have him find out where she was, and that she was literally only a couple hundred miles down the road from him, would hurt her dad more than she'd been doing for the last nine years. He might even come here...if her mother let him, that was.

The last time she'd talked to him, she'd been in the forest of the Buxa Tiger Reserve in India. She'd been in her tent going over some of the pictures she'd taken that day, and thought of calling him. It wasn't their usual call day, and she was surprised when her mother answered the phone.

The cell phone that they'd exchanged all those years ago had long since been broken, but she'd picked up a phone that could go for days without a charge, and it was pretty hard to break. Even a rhino walking over it hadn't busted this one. And like most of the time, there had not been anywhere to charge this one, which had been charged a few weeks ago, but it was still going. It was not often that there was running water where she was, much less electricity.

"Mom, it's Ramsey. Your daughter." There was a long pause and she thought her mother had hung up. "I just wanted to see how you're all doing. How is Deidra—?"

"I'll get your father. I don't have time to speak with you today. Not that I'd make the time anyway. I think you've done enough damage to this family as it is." When the phone was put down, Ramsey thought about just hanging up. It had been that way twice before when she'd called and gotten her mother instead of her dad. That day it had hurt her worse than before, because as she was waiting on her dad to come to the phone, she realized it was her birthday.

"Hello, Ramsey. How are you doing? Do you need anything?" Her dad asked her that every time he talked to her. "You've still not touched the money that I have put away for you to use. Whatever you're doing, does it pay you that well?"

"As a matter of fact, Dad, my needs are very limited. And I get paid very well for what I'm doing." She looked around her tent and smiled. "Very limited. Just what I can carry on my back, so to speak."

"I know what you're up to." He'd spoken so softly that she felt as if he was standing right next to her and had whispered in her ear. "It took me a while to figure it out, but I think I finally have it. You're out saving the world, aren't you? I know that sounds lame, but I just need to know that you're doing all right for yourself. Why don't you come home and tell me about it?"

Ramsey had thought of her mother and shook her head. "You know that I'd be about as welcome there as you would be where I am, Dad." She tried not to be hurt by her mother, but never wondered enough about her to think of reasons why Mom hated her. "You know, I could have talked to her. I tried to talk to her."

"I know. She's going through some things right now that have her upset. Deidra and her husband are coming to live here next month. I'm afraid that Chad has lost his job as well as a good portion of their money. I'd like to say that this is only temporary, but you know as well as I do that it's not." Ramsey thought of Chad Mosely and shivered. She had hated him on sight. "They don't have any children, thank goodness, but it will be hard on them coming here. Or maybe not. Deidra and her mother can spend more of my money. But with Chad… I'm going to lay down the law this time. No more paying off his gambling debts, and there won't be any spending money either. I've had enough of his crap. All of them, to be honest with you. I would love to see you again and complain face to face. Where are you?"

Ramsey could have told him about Chad had anyone asked her. Chad only married into her family to get to the money and to fuck the prom queen. Since her sister wasn't putting out without a ring on her finger, he'd married her. But something that Chad didn't know, and she was pretty sure Deidra didn't either, was that the money would never be his. It was all tied up so that no spouse would ever have access to the money, even in the event of death. Her dad was that good of an attorney, as well as a businessman. He said he dabbled in things. And he did that well too.

"So, when can you come home? Gregory is going to be here next week. And to be honest with you, I'd like to have someone I can complain to about him too. What do you think? It's been almost ten years, love. I miss you." Her eyes had filled with tears and she was ready to tell him she'd be home soon, but there was a man standing at her tent opening and he looked terrified.

"I can't right now, Dad. I have some things going on that I just can't walk away from." As she stood up after pulling on her boots, the man came into her tent. He was covered in blood, and she told her dad goodbye and ended the call. "What's happened?"

The knock at her hotel door startled her, bringing her

thoughts back to the here and now. Ramsey got up slowly, making sure that there wasn't any blood on her shirt, and made her way to the door. Looking in the peephole, she nearly groaned, but knew that the person on the other side would hear her and laugh, so she opened the door for him.

Godan was her friend. More than likely her best friend. He spoke very little, so when he did talk, she listened. They were the perfect pair when it came to working together. Neither of them had much to say, and even then they rarely said much.

"You will not like this so much after the hard ground, Missy." She nodded and pointed for him to come in. Once he was in he handed her a thick file, and then sat on the floor next to the thick cushioned sofa.

She'd been waiting on this file for two days. And now that it was here, she was almost afraid to open it. Sitting on the hard floor as he had done, she used the coffee table for her desk and opened it to the first page. Her breath caught when she saw the bus again.

"You healing?" Nodding at his question, she turned to the next page. "I think you lie. How long you going to suffer before you take yourself to the hospital? They are abundant here."

"They are, but I've no use for them now." She probably did, but only kept looking at the pictures. It was the fourth one that made her stop again.

The bus full of young children had fallen over the ravine where she'd been camped. There had been twenty-four children on the bus. No adults other than the driver, and he'd been dead long before he'd driven them over the cliff. The gunshot to the back of his head had killed him instantly.

Godan had been out walking and had seen it coming down the steep cliff. Children had been falling from the broken windows when he'd run to get her.

As soon as she arrived, Ramsey started taking pictures. Not just of the wreckage, but of the children as well. The blood on Godan's shirt was from a child that had spilled out nearly into his arms. And by the time she'd crawled into the bus to hand out one more child, she'd been just as covered.

All but five of the children had been killed, either by the tumbling of the bus or being tossed out of it when it had rolled. Ramsey had had no time to think about what might have happened then; it was all she could do to help save what few they could. The bus was rocking even after it stopped rolling at the embankment. It was only seconds from rolling off and into the fast moving river.

"Three have gone home. Two more dead." Ramsey asked Godan if the other bodies had been claimed yet. "Not sure. They will not let my kind in, so we are having to bribe who we can." She nodded and told him to let her know if he needed more money. He said that he had plenty for now.

"How much?" He didn't answer her so she paused to look at him. "How much did they offer you to keep your mouth shut?"

"Ten thousand. I took it. We can use the money." She nodded. "We have pack in the office building now. Things will come to us better."

Nodding again, Ramsey finished looking at the photos. There were more, she knew that, but right now, these were the ones that she needed. When she stood up, so did Godan, and he followed her into the kitchenette, where she'd put on

35

a pot of water for tea.

"I'll write up what I can today and get it back to you. I'd like for you to stay here. There is plenty of room." He just shook his head. "I've met the alpha bitch today. Go to them, but do not tell them we know each other, all right?"

"She will know." Yes, she supposed that this woman would know. "There are nine with me. I have put them in the wooded area close by should you need them."

"Thank you. And so you know, I don't think we'll be here all that long. I have…I want to get back out there and get to work. I'm sure you understand." He nodded. "Let's make a plan to leave here after the gallery opening. Oh, and Margo is coming, so make sure you stay back from her. You know that she wants you in her bed." He laughed and so did she.

After he left she sat back on the floor. Pulling up her laptop, she started the program to keep her safe, as well as the men that had come with her. No one knew who she was when she sent out these kinds of pictures, and no one ever would. So far as anyone knew, she was a ghost. And that was all they knew her by. Ghost was well known now for what was printed in her father's papers.

The pictures that you see before you are that of a murder. Not just the man with a bullet in his head, but the children as well. There is no end to what people will do for the almighty dollar. Have a child kill a man for gain….

Ramsey wrote for nearly three hours, never going back over what she'd written. She wouldn't do that until she was finished. And once she made sure there was nothing in the article to give her away, she would send it, along with the pictures, to the newspaper she'd been dealing with, the only one since she'd started this. The editor would receive her article through her dad, and he'd make sure it wasn't altered in any way. It was their deal. He'd even come up with the small ghost that accompanied each of her bylines. But even her dad had no idea that the man behind "Ghost" was his very own little girl.

After it was complete she sent it, along with the contents of the thumb drive that the pictures had been printed from. Godan had gotten really good at using their darkroom, and she thought about giving him a raise. But that wasn't really going to happen. She knew he wouldn't take it if she did offer. He was a man of very little material needs. Even less so than she was.

But a hot shower and a thick steak sounded so good right now that she turned on the water to its hottest setting and ordered her meal. She had approximately thirty minutes to bathe before it got there.

Getting out of the shower, then eating a meal that wasn't as good as she'd had in her mind it would be, she pulled the sleeping bag from the closet and laid it out on the floor. She supposed she could have used the bed, but it wasn't to her liking. First of all it was soft, and the second thing was, she didn't care for sleeping in someone else's bed. She was odd like that.

Laying down naked, as she liked to sleep, Ramsey closed her eyes and tried to will all the pain in her body to simply disappear. It wouldn't, but one could hope, she supposed. Sleep was long in coming, but when she did drift off, she thought of her dad once more. He would hate her if he ever found out who she'd become and why.

CHAPTER 2

"I can't tell you." Addie wanted to tell them all what she knew, but there were lives at stake. She wasn't entirely sure how many, but it would be Ramsey that would be hurt the most. And Graham would surely die defending her. "What I can tell you is that she's not in any sort of trouble that will harm any of us. But she does have secrets. Lots and lots of them. Don't pry. I know that's like waving a red flag in front of you, Hunter, but in this, you have to listen to me. She won't do any of us any harm if we let things play out the way we should."

"Does she belong to Graham?" It was an odd way to put it, but she told Hunter that she did. "Then we have to protect her."

Addie growled low. "She does not need us to protect her. Trust me on this. She can call in an army if she needs them. From all over the world, wolf and man alike would come to her aid. It's not her I'm protecting, but Graham."

"A man by the name of Godan came to see me this morning. Is he helping her in any way?" Addie had no idea and said so. "He doesn't talk much, very little as a matter of fact, but he said that there were ten in all and that they'd come to see me when they were settled. I assumed they were in the hotel, but there is no one registered there but this Ramsey person."

"Graham and Ramsey are...they're more than suited for each other. They both have things in their lives that will... they'll need each other to work through them. Not a life or death situation, but just things that will arise from them being together." Hunter asked her if she meant the things that Graham did. "Yes. As a matter of fact, with her help he'll be able to do things he's not been able to do. And the same with her. He will be a person in her life that will make what she does work out better and faster, and don't ask me what it is because right now, all I know is that she is very important to a great many people."

"You're only making me want more information; you know that, don't you?" Addie sat down and nodded. "I suppose if I asked Shawn or Luke to look into her, I'd be messing up things for them?"

"No. What you're going to find is that Ramsey Holms doesn't exist at all. And the man that you know her to be is R. S. Holms, who is a recluse that no one has met before. Most think that she's a male, just as you did. Her photographs have graced the front of countless magazines, but not her picture. There has not been a single word printed about her since she had her first picture put on the front of the newspaper almost nine years ago." Hunter started to pace and Addie nearly laughed. "I know that you hate this, the not being aware, but trust me when I tell you, you're going to save lives if you just stay out of it."

"That's the same as telling him to push full speed ahead and damn the consequences, you know that don't you, darlin?" Addie smiled at Cash as he walked in the room. "Remember how he was with you, Sloan, my dear? Just would not listen to his old man, and what did that get him? Nothing but heartache. It took me to smooth things over, or I'd not have the apple of my eye. Where is little Lea? Napping?"

"Yes. And please don't wake her. She's had a fussy night, and I think she's tired." Cash looked so disappointed that she wanted to take him to the nursery herself. But Addie knew that little Lea needed her rest. The poor thing hadn't been sleeping well, and neither had her parents.

"I met me an angel today. I swear to you, prettiest thing you done ever did see." He winked at her, then Sloan as Cash continued. "Can't hold a candle to the two of you, but she sure is a pretty little thing. Quiet too. Not saying a word about nothing to nobody. But she was seeing a lot. I could tell that."

"What do you mean, Dad?" Cash shrugged and looked at Hunter like he was trying to think how to tell him. "Did you happen to…what am I saying? You did get her name. Who is she?"

"Don't know for sure. I think someone called her Homes, but can't be sure. She had an older wolf with her. Big man that looked like he'd cut your throat out of you before he'd let you get near her. But I did say hi to her, and she nodded right back with this smile that made me think of angels." Addie watched Cash as he thought before speaking. He knew more than he thought he did. "She reminds me of somebody. Can't be sure who it is right now, but it'll come to me."

Addie looked at Hunter when she was sure that Cash didn't have it yet. "Leave Ramsey alone and things will go just fine. I promise you this. Graham will meet her in due time, and when he does, it will be good. I swear to you."

"And if I tell you that I can't leave this alone? That I worry too much because you won't tell me what you know, that I'm going to look into this anyway?"

Addie stood up and moved to the door before answering Hunter. "Then all hell will break loose, and you will reap the consequences of your work. And the deaths—and there will be more than you can know—will be upon your head." She moved out of the house and to her car. He would do this, despite what she'd told him. Hunter was a good man, but he was stubborn too.

Before she could get her key in the ignition, her passenger door opened and Cash slid in beside her. "She's Ramsey Stockholm's daughter, ain't she?" Addie nodded but said nothing. "Looks like her mother did when she was younger. It wasn't until I heard her first name that I remembered it all. You did that on purpose, didn't you, darlin?"

"She's not going to be happy that you know her. Even less so when she finds out about Graham. She's used to being alone." Cash nodded. "Not like Graham is used to it. He still comes to see his family. Ramsey hasn't seen hers in almost ten years, and I don't think she has any plans of opening that avenue any time too soon."

"I won't call him. Her daddy, he's a good man for all intents and purposes. A bit stuck up when he thinks he needs to be, but him and me, we were friends once. His wife—her name is Krista, I think—she's not one I'd want to tangle with, either as my wolf or myself. You know them?" Addie nodded. She had gone to college with Deidra's husband. And she knew that Graham knew him as well. Chad Mosley got around, and not in a good way. "I'll talk to Hunter. Won't do much good, I don't think, but I'll have a talk with him. Think I might have a sit down with that big wolf of hers, too."

"Tread lightly with him, Cash. He's very protective of her. She saved his life once and he owes her that. A life for a life." Cash nodded and looked out the window to the house. "Don't do it. Just don't play matchmaker. He'll find her in time."

"Yeah, I know you're saying that. But the big part of me wants to see my Graham happy. I don't think he has been in a long while." He hadn't, but Addie said nothing. "You go on about your business and I'll do mine. I won't interfere unless it comes to that."

He'd be talking to them both before the end of the day, she just knew it. After he left her car, she drove into town. There were things she could do to make things work out better. The first thing Addie did was go to see her grandmother. She would have the best ideas, and Addie missed her. Going up the front steps to her grandmother's new home, Addie had to smile. Things were going to be just wonderful when all was said and done. And she could not wait for them all to be happy again.

~~~

Graham moved along the bank of the water and watched eddies move along the branch. He knew that he had to dislodge it, but getting into the water without his wet suit would be freezing. And even if he could move the branch away from the shelter of the muskrats that were living in it, there was no guarantee that he'd not disturb the home too much for the little ones inside.

"I can swim." Graham turned so quickly that he nearly fell over his equipment. The man standing behind him put out his hands as if he was showing him he was harmless. But Graham thought that was about as far from the truth as anything could ever be. "I can help you, yes?"

Graham had no clue why, but he trusted the man. When he smiled, Graham thought of monsters in the dark. Not that this man was one of them, but he would be the one that came out of the shadows to swing the sword to vanquish them. Graham shook his head on such nonsense.

"I have to be careful of the animals that live inside the barge they have." He nodded as if he understood. "Swimming against this current will be difficult, to say the least. You have to be able to swim better than in a pool."

"I can swim well." As if to prove his point, the man took off his shirt and shoes, tossed his money and a cell phone on the clothing, and dove into the water. When he came up about a foot or so from the branch, Graham grinned.

Graham stripped down as well and dove in further up the water. When he came up for air, he was about ten feet from the branch and on the opposite side of it. He looked at the man across from him.

"I'd like to be able to lift it up over the nest, but I'm not sure how much of it is under water." The man nodded. "We can do this, you think?"

"We are strong. Yes, we can do this."

His confidence was great, and when Graham reached

out to the part of the limb that was closest to him, he lifted it up, surprised to see that it was not much bigger than the part that he could see. Lifting it up, they had it over the barge and floating down the river in no time. Not a word had been spoken since he told them they could do this. It was as if they were on the same page of a very good book.

When they got out of the water, the big wolf of a man shook all over. His hair seemed to make small rainbows all over the sand they were standing on, and when he reached for his shirt, Graham saw the scars.

Someone had beaten this man nearly to death at one time. And while the wounds were healed, he doubted very much that the pain of it had ever gone away. He wanted to ask him, but didn't want to have the man upset with him. Graham had so few friends, and he thought this man would be a good one.

The man turned to him then and caught him staring. "It is not a problem now. She has taken care of me well."

"Who?" The man only nodded and smiled again. "I'm Graham Emerson. I want to thank you for your help and pay you for it. I would have had to have someone come and help me had you not."

"No need for payment. I have had fun." He pulled his shirt over his wet body. "My name is only Godan. I have no last name."

"You're not from around this area, are you?" He told him that he was not. "My family lives around here. My brother is the alpha. Have you spoken to him yet?"

"I have. He is a good man. The others, the men with me, they will see him too, soon." Godan started to leave, and Graham called him back. "You will do well, Graham Emerson.

45

You are a good man as well."

When he disappeared into the woods, Graham stood there feeling slightly off. He felt like he'd been given a gift of something, but was not sure what it was or how it would affect him. But he felt good, better than he had for a long time. Pulling on his clothes, he paused and looked at the fast running water again. The man had nearly done all the work himself, and Graham had a feeling that had he not been there to help him, Graham would surely have been hurt. Shaking off the crazy notion, he finished dressing and made his way to his truck. It was time for him to get going again.

Graham liked the fact that he had his house completed now. He could come and go as he pleased, which he supposed he did before, but now no one was around to ask him where he was going. Today he was headed to town. He had to get himself something to eat for the rest of the week, plus he had to check his mail. No one would deliver it to his house because he was so far off the beaten path.

As he pulled up in front of the store, he saw his dad standing there talking to a young man. Graham got out, hoping to avoid being pulled into the conversation, but he knew his dad well enough to know that was never going to work.

"Graham, just the man I was hoping to see. This here is Matt. Matt, this is another of my sons, Graham. Matt here was telling me that he and a few members of his pack are hanging out at the old Derby farm. He was wanting to know if I knew the owners." Graham knew who owned it…he did. As of last month. "Said he and a few others were wanting to camp out or something out there. Do you know them? The owners, I mean?"

"There's a perfectly good hotel in town. You don't want to use it?" The man smiled but only shook his head. "You know a man by the name of Godan? I met him this morning."

"He said as much." Graham thought he wanted to say more, but only smiled again. Graham had a feeling that these men would outwit him in the lack of conversation department. "May we, sir?"

Graham nodded, and when Matt bowed and walked away, Graham looked at his dad. He was staring at him like he'd never seen him before. He asked him what he was doing.

"You own it, then?" Graham nodded, almost embarrassed to speak. "That man, Godan, you know him too? I met him, sort of, this morning. I think he's some sort of protection for this person with him."

"Today. We were working together in the river for a bit." His dad nodded and followed him into the store. "He said there were a few of them here in town. He never mentioned staying anywhere."

"How do you suppose he knew you owned the land? I didn't, and I pride myself on knowing it all." Graham knew that about his dad, and said nothing that was on the tip of his tongue about his dad being the nosey sort. "You coming out to the house tonight? I understand that it's the last meeting before they open the doors to the gallery. Nice young woman who paints has come in on the favor of that picture person."

"No. I have things to do around the house." His dad nodded.

There was nothing he needed to do around the house, and he was pretty sure his dad knew it. Picking up a bag of apples, he put them back. Then before he walked away, he put them in his cart. He didn't even care for fruits and vegetables on the whole, and yet looking in his cart he could see that in addition to the almost purchase of the apples, he had an eggplant and two heads of lettuce with a bag of tomatoes. Leaving them there so as not to have to explain to his dad why he was buying things he didn't eat, he made his way to the meat counter.

"You should come on out to the house tonight. You know as well as I do that you've been avoiding us. Why is that, I've been wondering?" He didn't answer his dad because while it was true, he had no answer either. "There might be some people out there for you to connect up with."

He paused in tossing the steaks he'd chosen into his cart and stared at his dad. "Who? Who might be there that I can connect up with? Dad, if you're playing matchmaker again, I will move away without telling you where I've gone. I swear to you."

"Don't have nobody that wants to come around you anymore. You done fixed that right up, didn't you? I'm just saying that there are some new people in town that you might want to talk to. You surely don't talk to none of us anymore." Again it was true, but he had his own demons to deal with and none of them could help him with it. At least he never thought they could. "You should come out."

"No, and hell no." The hit to the back of his head reminded him that not only was he nearly thirty years old, but his father treated him like he was still ten. "Dad, don't you think we're a little old for you to beating in the back of the head? I certainly hope we all are."

For his question, he was bopped in the head again. "When

you start acting like you got more sense than a jackrabbit, then I'll stop hitting you in the back of the head. Might still be able to knock some sense into you, but I'm doubting it after all this time." Graham said nothing, but smiled inwardly. He'd heard his dad say the same thing to Luke a while back when he told them that he was going to retire from the mayoral position. "I'm expecting you at the house. Not going to take no more excuses on how you got things to do. Your house has been done for a month now, and we'll have you coming over again. You hurt them grandbabies of mine when you don't show. Wouldn't be so bad if you were to contribute to the group of them, but I'm guessing you have to find a mate for that to happen. You haven't, have you?"

"No, I haven't contributed to your grandchildren. I'd let you know if I had." This time the hit to his head made his neck pop. And as his dad moved off, talking to himself about ungrateful children and no grandbabies coming in, Graham moved to the fresh vegetable area again to put his weird purchases away.

He might not have noticed the man standing by the door with a small blue shopping basket in his hands had it not been for the woman. She stood there looking to him like a small child that had lost her way. Graham didn't move toward the couple right then, but he could tell that she was very upset. And the man with her wasn't sure what to do. As he made his way to the cash registers, slowly pushing his cart like he was looking for something, she looked directly at him and he stopped moving.

He had no idea what to think, and it took him several seconds to realize that he'd stopped breathing. When he moved from behind his cart to go to her, she seemed to come alive with fear and he stopped. There wasn't much in the way of physical distance between them, but it felt like oceans were separating them. Then the man that had been with her stepped between them.

"Don't." The man had been reaching for something at his back, but stopped when the woman spoke. "He's not who you think he is. He is a friend of Godan's."

"How do you know? I mean, I just met him today." She said nothing as the man moved back to stand beside her, but he never took his eyes from him. Graham had no doubt that if he were to step toward her again, he'd be a dead man. Whoever she was, he was going to keep her safe. "I won't hurt you. Never that."

"He will kill you if you try, so I'm not concerned that you will." Graham nodded and took a small step toward her again. "I don't know what you think you're about to do, but I'd think hard on it if I were you. I'm not your friendly type."

"No, I don't think you are. But you're beautiful. Very much so." She said nothing, but backed up when he took another step toward her. The man moved, but Graham did nothing more than look in his direction. It had the man dropping to his knees and keeping his head low rather than reaching for the gun that he could now see. He looked at the woman again. "I won't hurt you."

"Don't do this. You have no idea what you might be doing right now." He told her he was pretty sure she was his mate. "I might be, but we can't act on it."

"Why not?" He was within touching distance of her now. A mere few inches from feeling her skin as much as he wanted.

"I need to touch you. Just enough to know for sure. All right?"

"No, I don't think that's a good idea." He nodded and reached out his hand slowly. "You're not listening to me. I need you not to touch me."

"I heard you. And so far you've given me no reason to not want to touch you." He brushed his fingers over her soft cheek, and knew in that moment what his wolf was telling him was right. "You're her. My mate. Would you mind...I mean, can I kiss you? Now? I need to taste you."

"Your parents, did they teach you that no means just that?"

He nodded and moved his body to touch hers to his. His wolf growled at him to touch her more, and he could have sworn that she felt it too the way that she stared at him. When she started to back away, he reached to wrap his arms around her waist, and nearly fell back when she screamed.

Graham started to release her but realized that she was unconscious. Holding her as gently as he could, he looked at the man that had been with her. He nodded once and waved for him to follow. Graham didn't even hesitate, but went out of the store with him and into the awaiting van parked right outside. Godan was driving and turned to wink at him as he settled in the seat. For the rest of the ride, he held onto his mate and wondered what the hell was going on.

CHAPTER 3

Ramsey woke to the sound of shuffling feet. It was a sound she was familiar with, but not one she was happy to hear. Sitting up a little in the short hospital bed, she wasn't surprised to see Godan there, but the stranger she was surprised to see. Looking at her friend, he smiled at her before speaking.

"You fainted." Ramsey only nodded at Godan. "He has not left your side since you were brought here. The hospital has no knowledge of who you are, and I have not told him either."

"Does he know what happened to me then?" The man in question sat up on the chair he'd been sleeping in and smiled at her. "What are you doing here? Whatever you think you are to me, you should just forget it. I have my own people to care for me."

"I'm sure you do, but Godan and I have a special interest in you, so we stayed. He said that he owes you his life, and I am your mate." He grinned again. "You were pretty before, but now you're just simply gorgeous."

"Where are my clothes?" Ramsey didn't want to think

about the man who grinned like a small boy on Christmas morning and made her feel warm all over when he winked at her. He was much too big, for one thing, and she thought he might be right in the mate department of their *not going to happen* relationship. When she asked again about her clothing, she looked at Godan. He was grinning at her as well.

"You should rest. I have much to tell you." When she laid back down, suddenly terrified of all the things that could be going on right now, she looked at the man again. But Godan spoke again. "His name is Graham. He is the alpha's brother. You have talked to his brother's mate today."

"So?" Graham didn't sit down on the chair again but on the bed with her. Ramsey didn't know what to think about him being so close, so she tried to only think about Godan. "What's going on beside this? What's happened?"

"He's trying his best not to tell you that my dad knows who you are. Who you really are. Dad came in here about an hour ago about to rupture something, and I told him what you were to me. He said that no one should call your parents just yet. I let him think I knew what he was talking about and he spilled it out. You're Ram Stockholm's daughter, aren't you?" She had to leave. Looking at Godan, she could see that he thought the same thing. "You're not going anywhere. I can't let you."

"You *can't* let me? And how the hell do you suppose that's going to work out for you? In the event you didn't get it before, I don't want you in my life. I have no need for you, nor — and this is a big one — nor do I think it will benefit either of us if you are in my life. I like being alone."

"As do I." He took her hand into his, and she noticed that

54

while she'd always thought of herself as a big person, next to him she was tiny. His one hand was as big as her entire head, she thought. "But you have some issues concerning your wounds that need attention. Can you tell me what happened?"

She looked at Godan again, and was afraid when she realized that he'd left her. He wouldn't be far, she knew that, but she didn't want to be left alone with this man. He asked her again what had happened.

"A school bus full of children, most of them dead, was going over into the river. We had to work pretty fast to get the living out. Once they were out, Godan and I went back in to get the dead. No one was going to be washed away." She expected him to tell her that she was a fool for going after ones that could not be saved, but he only nodded. "The bus moved just as I was...I nearly lost her, but Godan pulled her from my arms just as the bus was taken under."

"You were inside when it went over." Ramsey nodded. "And did you know that you have three broken ribs, as well as some bruising to your kidneys?"

"I figured as much. But there's not a lot of doctors where I work." He nodded as if he understood her. "I'd like my clothing now, please."

"All right." He stood up and Ramsey felt both cold from the loss of his heat and terrified that he'd been able to get her to talk about something that still made her have horrific dreams. "My dad said to tell you that he'd take your secret to the grave. I told him that I'd put him there should he speak of you to anyone. I wanted him to know how serious this was. I think I might have frightened him a bit. My dad is not one to take a threat lightly, but he did tell me he understood."

"You should tell him you're sorry. You never know when something might happen to either of you and you can't go back and fix it." She flushed when he turned to stare at her from the open closet. "I did the same thing, as you might have guessed."

"Your father?" She nodded, not really sure why she was telling him anything. "I have some things for you to wear. They're not yours. When you were brought in they had to cut things away and…I have a shirt of mine for you to wear, and a pair of old shorts that are going to be too big for you. Godan wouldn't breech your room, as he called it."

"So, I'm free to leave?" He said nothing and Ramsey sensed a trap. "Where is it that I'm going to go? I'm assuming that you've made some sort of deal with the hospital to allow me to leave, even though they don't want to."

"I did. They know me and my family. I'm taking you to my home. And before you get all worked up about it, it's a big house and I won't be sleeping with you. Yet." It was the yet, softly spoken, that made her body warm up. "You do know that I can smell you, don't you? And I can smell when you're aroused, as you are now."

"I just want my clothing."

He nodded and went to her. They were in his hand but not where she could just take them. Again she sensed she was in trouble, but had no idea what sort. When he lowered his head to hers, Ramsey licked her lips. The thought of this man kissing her, if that was his intent, was all she could think about when his mouth hovered just above hers.

"Do you know what I want from you?" Her head was nodding before her mind could work out how to answer his softly spoken question. "I want all of you, Ramsey. To taste you right now, it would be only the beginning."

"I don't know what I want, but I need for you to kiss me. I need it more than I need to breathe." She felt his little puff of laughter as it burned onto her mouth. "Kiss me, Graham, please?"

As soon as his mouth took hers—and it was a taking, not a kiss—she knew that for as long as she lived, this would be the one memory that she'd hold dearest to her heart. The first time in her life that she came alive.

His mouth was everywhere. Along her throat, nibbling at her ears. When he moved down her neck to her breasts, his hand cupped her tightly but gently as he nipped at her through the gown. Suddenly, even before she could protest that his mouth had stopped doing such amazing things to her, her breast was bare and he was suckling on it.

Her body laid back on the bed, his hands roamed over her until she knew that she was naked. As she lay there, her body exposed to his eyes, she started to cover herself when he didn't say anything but just stared at her. It wasn't until he put his hands over hers that she looked at his face.

"Please don't. I want to see you. I need to see you."

Nodding, she moved her hands to the bed and gripped the sheet beneath her. She felt exposed, which was more to do with him not saying much than her being naked for him. His mouth moved to her navel and his tongue danced around it before foraging deep and making her body bow up off the bed. His mouth moved lower, his hands pulling her thighs apart as he feasted on her skin. When he licked at her pussy then sucked her clit into his mouth and bit down, Ramsey curled her hands into his hair and held on. She knew that when he touched her again, she was going to come apart.

The first climax that she had was quick, taking her breath away almost as soon as he sucked on her clit again. His body bent over hers, she held onto him, wondering what she could do to give him as much pleasure as he was giving her. Reaching down to his pants, she cupped his cock and heard him moan against her skin. The next time he touched her with his mouth, she nearly screamed when he sucked her clit into his mouth and nipped hard. Riding his mouth and his hands, Ramsey came twice more before she pulled him up with her hand fisted in his hair.

When he lifted his head from her she could see her juices on his chin and mouth, and thought it the most erotic thing she'd ever seen. The thought of what he'd done to be looking so delicious had her reaching for him. He backed away from her and told her not yet. Ramsey had no clue what she was doing, but her body seemed to so she let it do the thinking and talking for her. When she cupped her breasts, he moaned again, telling her not with words but his sounds that he was enjoying what she was doing.

Graham never took his eyes from hers as he stood up again and began to take off his shirt. His chest was slick with dew, his arms thick with muscles. All she could think about was what it would feel like to be fucked with so much power. His grin told her that he knew just what she was thinking.

"I'm going to be as gentle as I can, but I need to be inside of you. Now." Her head was nodding again, but her heart was telling her this was a mistake. This time her head won out when he pulled his pants off and stood before her as naked as she was. Christ, there wasn't anything about this man that made her think that he'd not give her his all.

His cock was as thick as her wrist, his length was hard, and the tip of him was leaking profusely. She wanted to taste him, take his cock into her mouth and drink down every bit of him, but he pulled her to the edge of the bed and picked her up so that she was wrapped around him. Locking her legs behind him, he moved them to the wall behind him and held her like this for several seconds.

"I'm afraid I'll hurt you. You've never had sex before, have you?" She shook her head and wondered briefly how he knew, but he nibbled at her breast again and she held him to her. It occurred to her that she knew nothing about this man, but it didn't seem to matter to her body. She needed him as much as he said he needed her.

His cock was at her entrance, and she wanted to pull him deep inside of her and feel him fill her. When he lifted his head this time, she could see his wolf. It was so close to the edge that she was sure she could touch him. He ordered her to kiss him, and when she took his mouth with her own, he slammed her down over his cock hard and fast. The pain of it was so incredible that she could only hold onto him for fear of screaming.

~~~

Graham held her to him. He didn't move, but he wanted to. To take her to the bed and lay her out and make her rest, but he knew as surely as he stood there with her crying in his arms that he'd not be able to do either of those things. Not until he came inside of her and had her bite him. The need to comfort her, the overwhelming need to make her his, was being pounded at him from the inside by his wolf. When she lifted her head from his shoulder, he called himself all kinds of a fool for hurting her. The tears on her cheeks made him think he'd never be able to ask for her forgiveness.

"I'm sorry. So incredibly sorry." Her nod and soft laugh had him pulling her chin around so that he could see her face. "What's funny?"

"I'm not sure. It just seems silly for you to tell me you're sorry with your cock still deep inside of me." He moved, he couldn't help it, and she moaned. "That feels wonderful. I'm not sure if you came or not, but I didn't. And I ache to come. Can you help me out?"

He moved again, this time as deep as he could while lifting her body up so that he could suckle at her breast while he brought her to the edge again. Her fingers dug deep into his shoulder and hair, and his wolf wanted the same thing, to be touched by her and held. When she started to ride him, push back with every stroke of his cock, Graham pounded her a little harder, took her faster. And when she came, crying out his name, Graham brought her twice more before he bit into her shoulder and emptied himself inside of her. But it wasn't enough...he wanted more, needed more from her.

Taking her to the bed, he didn't let her go but sat her on the edge while he moved inside of her. Watching his cock as it freed from her slightly, only to be buried again soaking wet with her juices, he was amazed at how much he wanted to fill her again. When she laid back, her body presented before him like a feast, Graham pulled from her and stood there until she looked up at him.

"My wolf wants to taste your pussy." He had no idea if

she consented or not, but he let his wolf take him. As soon as he was fully his animal, he moved to the bed and licked her pussy from gate to clit. Her fingers holding him to her was all the encouragement he needed to make a dinner of her.

She came three times, each time flooding his mouth and making him want more. His wolf hummed to him, telling him how pleased he was with his new mate. And when he licked her thigh, Graham knew that he would mark her gently but firmly. As soon as she cried out against the pain of it, his wolf whimpered but didn't let go until she was marked with his brand. Then Graham took his body back.

"You...he...." Graham laughed and told her yes. "I've never done that before. I've never even thought of something... is that normal for your kind?"

"I think so." Graham moved his mouth to her pussy and licked her just above her soft fur. "Now it's my turn." He could taste himself in her; his own come mixing with hers tasted good, and he wanted more. When she came again, her body bowing up off the bed, he slid his finger inside of her and brought her twice more.

She tasted of cream, the sweetest there was. Her body was hot, soft, and his. Graham tasted her with his tongue, sliding it inside of her over and over, drinking her down, and savoring her as much as he could. When she begged him to stop, telling him she couldn't take any more, Graham brought her again and again. Suddenly her hands in his hair brought him up instead of holding him to her.

"You're killing me." He grinned and pulled her to the edge of the bed. "No. No more. Please. I can't take any more."

"Yes, you can." He slid into her heat. She was slick and

swollen, and he fucked her slowly as her legs wrapped around his hips. "Come for me, Ramsey. Come hard and let me mark you too."

"No, please, no more."

He touched his finger to her clit, which was hard and peeking out of her nether lips like a beacon for him. When she came screaming his name, Graham leaned into her throat and bit down hard, bringing her with him once more as he emptied into her. His mate. She was his, and he had never felt as good in his entire life as he did at that moment.

Graham held her to him, his body more than spent, but never had he felt so alive. Lifting his head to make sure she was all right, he smiled when he saw her sleeping. He had never wanted or needed anyone as much as he had her. And if he was honest with himself, he wanted her again.

Lifting his body from her, she moaned slightly, but he was careful not to wake her. Picking her up as easily as he could, he settled her in the bed then pulled the gown back over her body. Just before covering her beautiful breasts, he nibbled on them again, just enough to have her moan, then covered them as well. He was gathering his clothing up when his brother, Hunter, touched his mind.

Where the hell are you? He told him. *I don't suppose you have Ramsey with you, do you? I've been...Christ, I have two people, two wolves from what I can only assume are her pack, here that need to speak to her right fucking now, and they're concerned that something might have happened to her.*

Is Godan there? Hunter said he didn't think so. *Hang on. He might still be here. And I do have Ramsey. I brought her here when I found out she was hurt.*

62

Graham might have told Hunter that she was his mate but didn't. They'd know soon enough. As he moved into the hallway, he saw the big wolf and told him what was going on. The man nodded once and left him.

I sent him to you. He'll fix things. I don't know what is going on, but I'm taking her to my house for now. She needs to rest. Hunter didn't say anything but he could almost feel his mind working. *Just ask.*

You've found her then. It wasn't a question but he answered him that he had. *Well, I'll be damned. We're all well and truly mated now. Does Dad know? Of course he does. I have no idea how that man finds things out so quickly, but he does. Worse than...I have to tell Sloan. I bet she knows too, but I'm still going to —*

Hunter? Hunter laughed when Graham cut him off. *I'm going to ask that you tell no one what you might know about Ramsey. She might be...I don't think she's in trouble, but she is running from someone.*

I can do that. I think...you think she'll be all right with you taking her to your house? He told him he had no idea, but that was where she was going. *Good luck with that, then.* Graham didn't know why, but he thought he was going to need all the luck he could get.

She slept for another hour, and when she woke up, Graham helped her dress. She didn't complain, but he knew that she was sore. Not just from her accident, but the sex too. He felt badly for taking her so many times...well, he sort of felt bad.

Ramsey didn't say much. He supposed it could have been from embarrassment, but he didn't think that was it wholly. She was quiet, as he was. Conversation was something that he felt you engaged in when you had something to say, not to empty your head. When she cleared her throat, he waited for her to speak before he did.

"We only met today and had sex. I'm not sure…I want to blame it on the drugs, but that's not it, is it?" He told her no. "So…will this happen a lot? Sex, I mean?"

"Yes. At least I hope so." He could barely contain his smile when she nodded. "We're wolves by nature, I think, and we're programmed to reproduce to have more of us. To keep the line going. That, and I find you to be incredibly sexy." He helped her out to his truck and into it before she spoke again.

"Will I have a baby? I mean, I know that babies turn into wolves later in their life, but am I pregnant?"

He wanted her to be. Graham wanted that more than anything, but knew that neither she nor him were ready for that just yet. "You're not in heat, so no." Nodding, she stared out the window and he drove them home. Home now would have an entirely different meaning than it had before meeting her. "The wolves that came with you, they're very protective of you. They will be with me as well now, did you know that? And Godan, is he their alpha?"

"I noticed that when we were at the store. I was…we were slightly overwhelmed by the store, I guess. I'd not been to a big kind of store like that in a few years. But to answer your question, Godan is their alpha of sorts. He brought them to my camp one night when…after…. He was being hurt, and I sort of took it upon myself to save him. He has been with me since. And the wolves came as his family. All of them are related in some way or another." Graham knew that. "They're not like you. Not dark. Godan and the others are special."

"How so?"

She didn't answer him, but again he wasn't surprised. There was no reason for her to trust him any more than he would expect her to do. As they pulled into the drive, he could see the wolves that hung around his property, all of them wild and friends of Sloan's. There were some on each of their lands now, each of them answering to Sloan first, then Hunter.

"You live here? Alone?"

Instead of answering her he got out and went to help her out of his truck. When she winced again, he picked her up in his arms and carried her to the door. It felt fantastic to have her arms wrapped around his shoulder, and he thought it was something he could get used to. If she didn't mind him carrying her everywhere.

His housekeeper met them at the door. She was a small woman, but she could beat bear with a switch, as his dad was fond of saying to him about her. Clara fussed over Ramsey and led him up the stairs to his room and helped him pull back the bed blankets. As soon as he put her on the bed, Clara said she'd get her something to wear as well as some nice broth, and left them alone again.

"She's a wolf too." Graham told her she was. "That's good. But you should know that Godan won't sleep in the house, but he will be close. Is that a problem?"

"He and the others have asked for permission to live on land that I own. It's not far from here, and they can have free run of it." He sat on the edge of the bed. "If you want a shower, I can help you."

"Will you join me?" Standing up, he reached for her and

led her to the large room. "I don't know why I'm taking this so well. It's not like me to do anything like this. Have sex with strangers, go to their house as if it's just fine."

"You're my mate." He pulled her into his arms and kissed her. He realized then it was his first for her. He'd kissed her during sex, but this was different, this one meant more than a prelude to sex.

Stripping his shirt and shorts he'd given her at the hospital off her by pulling the shirt up and over her head and dropping it on the floor, Graham thought he could get used to this very easily. The shorts, he knew, were going to be tricky in that he wanted to taste her again, and he wasn't sure if she was still sore from earlier. And when she cupped his cock, he rocked into her hand, wanting to bury himself deep inside her again. When his shirt was torn open, buttons going in every direction, he picked her up so that she was wrapped around him again.

"I need you." She nodded and rode his bared chest as he pulled at his pants. As soon as he was free, he pulled her over him, taking her as deeply as he could, and fucked her against the wall. Cupping her ass, bringing her closer to his body with every stroke, he nearly cried out when her mouth moved over his pulse at his throat. "Bite me, Ramsey. Take me into your body and bite me."

Her teeth tore at his flesh painfully. But he knew the moment she drew blood, the second that they were connected on a level no one else would ever breach. When she sucked hard on the wound, Graham bit into her shoulder, tasting the spice of her blood when she screamed her release around his flesh. Graham came too, his entire being filling her with everything that he was.

"You're mine." He nodded at her statement. Held her to him even as he kicked his pants off and toed off his shoes. "Please don't push me away, Graham. I don't think…I won't survive it again."

"Never. You're mine as well."

CHAPTER 4

Ram hadn't left the house in two days; he didn't want to miss her call. Ramsey called him every Sunday without fail, and now it had been two that she'd missed and he was more than a little worried. When Kent came in with a package, he nearly asked him if someone had called, but he answered before he could ask.

"No sir. She has not called. I have checked the phones to make sure there are no line issues as well. And the line that she uses to call you has been marked to not be used by the household." Ram nodded and took the package. "This is from the same handwriting as before, sir. Shall I call your editor and tell him that something is coming to him?"

"Yes. Please. And thank you."

He waited until his butler and only friend in the house was gone before he opened the package. This person, whoever it was, had been sending him these type of packages for the last five years, and without fail, it had been front page information that had hiked his circulation to nearly triple what it had been. And because of it, he was looking into other avenues to get the articles out in the public. The exposés had kept him afloat when all other print papers were folding. He looked at the letter before going to the file.

The pictures that you see before you are that of a murder. Not just the man with a bullet in his head, but the children as well. There is no end to what people will do for the almighty dollar. Have a child kill a man for gain? Yes, without any qualms about who else might be victimized by their action. An accident to happen so that you will have the eye of the world on you is nothing to these people, no matter who might die or who might live. But this time, their world was shattered when they sent a child to do a job for them that was doomed to fail from the start.

After reading it through twice, he set it aside and pulled out the file. There on the top was the driver of the bus that she had mentioned. And the next dozen pictures, all glossy eight by tens, were of the destruction of the children. Because there was no other term for what had happened to them, as well as the bus when it landed at the bottom of the dark ravine. It had settled next to a large, fast running river only to be sucked in by the current to land at the bottom of the falls in a twist of metal and blood. But the one of the dead children, all of them laying out in a neat row with another two or three of the living huddled next to them.... It tore at his heart so much that he had to lay it down and walk away for a moment.

Ram knew it was his daughter taking the pictures and writing the Ghost stories. He had no idea why he knew that. Sometimes he was terrified more than he was proud of her for what she was doing. But pride won out every time. When her work—and it happened more often than not—graced the cover of some big magazine, he would devour each word of what she had to say about her pretty pictures, and knew that his child had a darker side too. Her job was one that would get her into serious trouble should anyone find out what she was doing on the side that no one save him knew about.

The short knock at his office door had him cringing. It was either his wife or daughter, neither of which he wanted to talk to right now. But before he could say he was busy, Deidra came in holding a silk hanky to her face. *Here it goes again*, he thought.

"Daddy, Chad has refused to let me go into town to have lunch with Mommy. I have to go. They're having a sale on winter clothing, and I need so much now that I'm home again, and he's being mean to me. Mommy said she'd buy me a new outfit, but he wants me to go with—" He turned to look at her from his positon at the window. She was just picking up the last picture he'd looked at before he could tell her no. "Oh my God, Daddy. What is this? Are these people dead?"

She tossed it away from her as if she might catch something from it. He felt his temper rise up, something that had been happening more and more of late. Since right about the time she and Chad had moved back in.

"They are. And when you come into my office unannounced, you will have to take what you get." He picked up the picture, and out of what he could only think of as pure meanness, he showed her the one of the driver with the bullet in his head. "This one will be on the front page tomorrow."

Deidra ran out of his office screaming that he was mean to her as well. He was still laughing when his wife Krista came in. She was nearly boiling over mad, but right now he just didn't care. When she flopped down in the chair across from him, he waited. Usually he was the one that spoke first, trying to stem the tears or fight or both before she spoke. But he was feeling particularly nasty today and waited.

"Well?" He only cocked a brow at her. "What have you done now to upset your daughter? She came screaming to me just now that you were torturing her with pictures so that she'd have nightmares for the rest of her life. Why must you treat her this way? She's our only daughter."

"No, she's not. We have two. Remember? Ramsey is our daughter too. How can you forget that so often, I wonder?" Krista huffed at him. "I can't understand why you have to be reminded that we have another child. Perhaps you can enlighten me."

"Because we had our children. A boy for you and a girl for me. What the hell were you thinking telling me to keep the last one when I wanted nothing more than to abort her the moment I found out about it?" He'd heard this before, and it hurt no less for the amount of times he'd heard it. "Now that she's gone, and good riddance to her, we have moved on with our lives as she might have done with her own. I can tolerate the calls, so long as you never tell me again what she has to say. I just don't care, Ram. I never have. As far as I care, Ramsey was a mistake, and one that I have washed from my memory, thankfully."

"You're a sad, sad woman, Krista Stockholm. Why are you such a bitch about the one person…?" He shook his head, not even finishing the question. "You know what, I don't care. But know this…Deidra and Chad have one month to get their affairs in order and get out of this house, or I'll kick them to the curb. I like my peace and quiet, and I won't have them disrupting it every time they have a fight. Christ, they're worse than you and I are."

"You will not kick them out. So help me, if you do, then I'll leave you, Ram. I will." He didn't say anything, thinking that was even better news than he had hoped for. "You're not going to get me to stay if you do this. No matter what you try. I will not toss my daughter away like some unwanted guest."

"I won't even try." She sat there for several moments and he watched her. He'd gotten pretty good at judging her, and he knew as surely as he was sitting there that she'd no more leave him than she would miss a hair appointment. Not without a good hard shove, that was. He had the money, not her, and if she left him, she'd not get a single penny. He'd been preparing for this for years...nine years and nearly five months, really. And the pre-nup before that was perfect.

"You're not the same man I married, Ram. I don't care for this new you. I'd very much like it if you were to resume the way you were before." He told her no. "Then we are at a crossroads. I shall have to do something to bring you around."

"You do that and I will end everything that you have." She looked shocked. "There is nothing in your name, Krista. You signed that pre-nup when we married, and now, even after all this time, I will use it against you if you fuck with me. I'm rich; you are just my wife."

"You can't talk to me that way." Ram felt...well, he felt lighter for saying that to her, and when she stood up, so did he. "This is not you. You've been talking to Ramsey, haven't you? She's got you all worked up, and now you're taking it out on me. I won't have it, Ram. I'm not to be treated as less of a person. I'm your wife and the mother of your children, and you'll treat me as such."

"You mean like you treated Ramsey." He sat back down as he continued. "As we both did when she lived here. I followed your lead when it came to her, and I have regretted it every day since she left. I miss her more now than I ever did Deidra or Gregory when they moved out. And even less of Gregory. He is without a doubt the laziest man—no, the laziest thing—I have ever known."

"Well, they're home now, and we'll try our best to make things better for them. But I will not allow you to toss them out. We do have a standard to uphold. And if Gregory is lazy, that's your fault. As his father, you should have made him work harder. And those problems he has with drugs aren't as bad as everyone says they are." She moved to the door. "But if you even think of bringing Ramsey here, I will make your life a living hell, Ram. I promise you that."

When she moved out of the room, slamming the door behind her, Ram just shook his head. She'd been making his life a living hell for years now. It was only recently that he began to notice it rather than to ignore her.

When the phone rang he nearly sobbed with relief. But when he picked it up, it was to hear his son on the other end talking to Chad. The two of them had hit it off well since Chad had started dating, then marrying, his sister. He nearly hung up before he paused, hearing his name.

"Yeah, Dad has that car out there that we can take in if you want. He'd never miss it. I don't think he's been in the garage more than twice since I was born." Ram stilled, thinking about his vintage cars that he had there, and wondered if they had been taking anything before now.

"Just so we don't get caught. You sister is fucking driving me crazy about money all the time. She's like this leech that never gets enough blood. I tried to tell her that we have to pay off my debt first, but then she cuts me off. I need sex." Chad laughed bitterly. "Of course, paying for it is certainly better than I get for free from her. What a cold cunt she has."

Ram listened to them laughing and felt his temper start a low simmer. He was going to have to set his foot down. When they both hung up, after more shots at his daughter as well as him and Krista, Ram started writing out notes. The next thing he did was make a few calls. And within an hour, he had all the information he thought he needed. But his lawyer, Robert Shaw, said he could dig more when he called him.

"You do that. And as of this minute, all credit cards, including those for my wife, are cut off." He thought of the one that he'd given Ramsey all those years ago, and knew that she'd never once used it. Ram told him to keep that one active, just in case. He also mentioned to him some other things he wanted to happen and how.

"I think — and I don't know how to be delicate about this — but what about your will? Do you want to make any changes to it?" Ram smiled and told him yes. "Good man. I'll see you in the morning then. And so you know, I have sent a team of guards to keep an eye on your cars, as well as the warehouse you have downtown. You didn't mention that to me, but it does stand to reason that if they know about the cars, those antiques won't be very safe."

"Good. Good. One more thing. I have...can you find Ramsey for me? I've been waiting on her call for days now, and...I'm worried for her. Don't contact her, just let me know that she's all right. "He said he'd look, but she didn't leave much in the way of a print for him to follow. "That's my girl. When she said she was going to go where no one would know her, she did it up right."

After he hung up he called the paper. It was only one of his many investments, but this one was proving to be the most fun. Especially when he had a box from Ramsey. As he got things ready for the courier, he thought of his family. As soon as he had things set, the will as well as the rest of the things that he and Bob had talked about, he was going to have a long talk with them. One he was sure that they were going to hate. He was mentally rubbing his hands together as he made his way to his car. This one he knew no one had touched.

~~~

Graham was nearly to his barn when the police showed up. He didn't move. Not that he didn't know the chief of police personally, but they didn't look to him like they were here on a friendly type of a visit. He reached for Hunter even before the first man got out of the cruiser.

I think I'm in trouble. He asked him what was going on. *I'm not sure yet, but there are three very important looking men in suits coming toward me with flak jackets on and official looking papers. I don't know anything just yet. Max is with them, and he's pissed off.*

I'm coming. So is Sloan. I'll have her call Shawn too. He said that might be good. *What are they telling you? Graham?*

I'm trying to understand if you'd shut up. Graham put his hands up when the guy closest to him pulled out a gun. *I'm in some serious shit, and they've not even told me anything yet. Max is telling them to go easy, but that's not going to happen.*

"Graham Emerson?" He nodded, still watching the man

76

that was hanging back a little with his gun out too. "We'd like for you to come with us to answer a few questions about the deaths of Alison and Peter Anderson."

"I'm sorry, who?" Max told him who they were, and then he told the men to back the fuck off. "I don't know what you're talking about. I never met them before I found her body in the river. I didn't kill them."

"We just want to talk for now." Graham only nodded and was thrown against the wall of the barn like he'd done something wrong. "You'll not make it if you resist arrest, wolf boy."

Graham told Hunter what was being said to him. Then he heard the snap of someone close by and everyone around him stood very still. He was flipped around so quickly that it took him several seconds to get his balance. He saw Ramsey standing on the deck with her camera out. And when she started to move toward them, smiling, he could have kissed her.

"Don't mind me, boys. Go ahead and rough him up. I'm sure that it will play nicely on the six o'clock news how you came out and beat up an innocent man. What was it you called him again? I want to make sure I have it right when I call this in." She asked them for their names, and when no one said anything, she moved forward, her camera still pointed at them, taking pictures of where their name plates should have been, and then of the blank badge cases that hung from small lanyards. "You guys aren't local, either. I don't even think you're Feds, though you want to be. Are you?"

"You can't record us. It's against the law." She told him it wasn't and asked for his name again. "I'm not going to give it to you, so fuck off."

"Nasty mouth you got there, buddy. Do you kiss your boyfriend with that mouth?" He growled at her and Graham felt his wolf move angrily against his skin. Then he felt the man holding him grip his arms tighter behind his back. He stiffened before Ramsey spoke again, this time with humor in her voice. "I would not do it if I were you. You might hurt one or two of them, but they'll have you for dinner before you shot all of them."

Graham looked to where the men who had come with Max were staring. Max was laughing, but the rest of the men were not. And not one of them moved when the biggest white wolf he'd ever seen walked toward him and his captor. The others, about two dozen more white wolves, went to stand next to Ramsey. He knew right then that this was what she'd meant when she said that Godan and his family were special.

"You can't have wild animals running around here. There is a law about that." The man still holding him was apparently in charge, or he thought he was as he moved with him toward the cruiser. "You call them off right now and I won't have a warden come out here and round them up."

"Release him or I'll turn them on you." Ramsey's voice was low but there was no doubt that she would do just as she said. When the wolf next to him rubbed his head on the man's leg, he screamed like he'd torn his leg off. The gun going off so close to his ear had Graham crying out in pain.

If anyone was shot, Graham couldn't tell from his position on the ground. The big wolf was laying over him, and the men that had come with Max were scrambling to their car. Graham put his hand on the big wolf's back and he moved off him, but didn't go far. The others were surrounding Ramsey as if she were their queen.

When he was standing again, thanks to the hand up that Max gave him, he looked around the yard. The wolves were there, black ones standing just on the edge of his property like they were ready for battle. The white group had their fur standing on end and their teeth showing as they growled low in the backs of their throats. He looked at Max when he said his name.

"I'm powerfully sorry, Graham. I didn't know what they were doing. Said they had some questions for you and nothing else. It was a surprise to me when that one fellow pulled this stunt. I'm going to be making me some calls when I get back to the office. You okay, boy?" Graham told him he was. "Tell Hunter when he gets here I'll be back. I just thought they were asking you questions, and now this."

"I understand."

Graham didn't, but he watched the older man walk to his car. The men inside were all on their phones, and Graham had a feeling it wasn't going to bode well for him. As soon as the car was gone, Ramsey came to him and wrapped her arms around him. He held her too.

"You said they were special." She looked up at him. "The wolves, you said they were special. I had no idea they were snow wolves. Where did you find them?"

"I didn't find them so much as inherit them when Godan was hurt. They're his family. Godan's family. And they've been with me since Godan said he wasn't leaving me. He sort of thinks he owes me his life."

"He said you saved him." Ramsey pulled away and he

pulled her back. "Not yet, please. I need to touch you. What did you do? How did you save him? Please, I'd like to know."

"They were beating him. To make him shift. They were…I think they were going to skin him for his fur. As you said, white wolves are very rare, even for shifters. I don't know how many other times they'd done this or what other shifters they had killed, but they were taken care of." Her shiver made him reach for her again, and she leaned against his chest as she continued. "He'd been tied to a long pole and his family, his wife and child, were there as well. The little boy was dead before I came upon them, but Godan's wife, Mary, had been brutally raped several times. I wasn't sure if she'd make it, but…." She looked out over the field to where the others had gone when the cruiser had left. Ramsey continued as if remembering the time like she was still there. "I moved in much like I did today, with my camera going. But they didn't know that I'd set up a recording one a few feet from us. If I died helping him, I wanted someone to know why. Almost as soon as he was free, the wolves attacked the men and tore them apart. I…it was the first time that I'd seen such a display of protectiveness. And something that I've come to realize is in their nature as much as being a wolf is."

"Where were you when this happened?" If she heard him, she didn't answer him. Graham watched her relive the memory before she finally continued.

"I had to work quickly. Before I could even get the first of the chains off him, I knew that he wasn't going to make it. While the others, the wolves, had their…they made them pay once I got their leader out of harm's way." Graham knew there was more, but he wasn't sure he wanted to hear any more than she was telling him now. "Mary died. It was a few days later that she just bled out. The wolves never left us as I cared for him. He should have died as well, I suppose, but the pack, his pack, wouldn't have survived without him, and I told him that every hour of every day."

"You cared for him when the others tried to kill him. No wonder he and the others are so loyal to you." She turned then and looked up at him. "I'm falling in love with you, Ramsey."

"I know. But...what are we going to do now?" He wondered if she meant with him loving her or something else. "I can't tell you that I love you, Graham. I don't know what it is to love or to be loved. My family is so fucked up that... well, if you ever met them, you'd understand completely. But what do we do now? I have to go back in the field soon, and you have your own job to do. Then there are those people hell bent on making you pay for a crime that you did not commit. Where does that leave us?"

"I don't know, love. I just don't know. But they'll come back, and I have a feeling that when they do, it will be to arrest me for sure. I didn't kill those people. I just found their bodies." He was glad to hear her say she believed him, because that had been a terrifying thing that had just happened to him. Hunter pulled into the drive just as Graham was going to suggest they go back up to their room and make love until they couldn't walk.

"I just spoke to Max. He's fit to be tied. Never heard a man so worked up before about his job." Hunter pulled him in for a heavy handed hug. "You're all right then? No need for us to call in the cavalry?"

"Not just yet. But they're going to take me in for the

murder of those two people. And soon too. Hunter, I don't understand why they even think I did this." Hunter looked at Ramsey, then at him again. It was comical to see him looking so confused. "She's my mate."

"No kidding." Hunter put out his hand to Ramsey and Graham wasn't sure she was going to take it. When she did, Graham wanted to hug her to him again. "Welcome to my family. I really thought he'd come by sooner to introduce you to us."

"Nah, I think he didn't do that on purpose. You seem like the nosey type. Maybe he and I just wanted some quiet time together. And he figured you'd have to be all up in his ass about it." Hunter stared at Ramsey like he could not believe she'd spoken to him like that. Then Sloan laughed and welcomed her to the family as well. When the two women went into the house, Hunter looked at him again.

"She's going to fit right in, you know that, right?" Graham said nothing, but he had to agree. There was nothing about her that made one think she was going to be a pushover. "I like her. But what happened here? Max said that they showed up at his office this morning saying they wanted to talk to you about the woman's body. He told them that you'd also found the man out there that had turned up a few weeks ago. Max said he never even thought that they'd jump to conclusions that you were a part of their deaths. But he did get a kick out of the way that Ramsey messed up their plans. Did he tell you who they were?"

"Yeah, he said their names were Alison and Peter Anderson. I don't think I knew them, do you?" Hunter said that he didn't. But he'd find out. The women came out of the house then, and Graham could see that Ramsey was a little upset. But Sloan was bullying her into the car even as she waved goodbye to him. He started to go to them when Hunter stopped him.

"They're going to the gallery, I guess. Ramsey's artist friend showed up and Sloan is dying to meet her. Not to mention, Ramsey's work is drawing some pretty good attention and has some newspapers hanging around. I'm guessing this thing is going to be bigger than anyone thought it would be." Graham wondered why Sloan didn't just go on her own, but Hunter only shrugged. "I guess it's a girl thing. I don't have a clue. And now that you have your own mate, you'll understand just how true that statement is."

CHAPTER 5

Ramsey watched Sloan. She was the perfect woman. Strange that she'd always thought of her sister and mother that way when she'd been at home. But to see it, know firsthand that this was the way a woman acted, made her want to hunt down her family and have them see what she was seeing. Gentle and kind when she needed to be, and just as firm and hard when the occasion called for that as well. When Sloan turned to her, Ramsey just stood there, thinking that if she was smart, she'd run for cover. There was something very scary about this perfect woman too.

"Jack and the rest of my sisters are coming into town to meet you. We'll all have dinner at my house, and then we'll talk about how badly this grand opening is going to go in a few days." Ramsey looked around the room and the changes that she'd suggested being put into fruition. "You helped me a great deal, Ramsey. It really would have fallen apart if you'd not come in to help. The teenagers are excited about working it, and Addie talked the school into giving them extra credit if they wrote something up on the art that they were assigned to. The food is going to be served by them as well. And the local shop that rents tuxedos at prom time is letting them use them for free if we put their name on the back of the program. I can't thank you enough for telling Clemmie that you'd help us."

"Mrs. Mantel is a good friend. When she contacted my lawyer, I told her I'd come and help out. I needed a break anyway. Not that she'd take no for an answer, but I have learned to pick my battles with her. It's easier." Ramsey was still trying to figure that one out. Of course the woman had some freaky powers. "Her family and mine knew each other. I'm not sure if that was a good thing or not. My mother, of course, hated her after Clemmie told her that she was a snob and not the slightest bit genuine. The fun part of that was, Clemmie loved my dad."

"Clemmie can be very nasty when she feels that something is wrong. And if she likes you, doors tend to open that wouldn't before." Ramsey knew that as well. Although she'd never had the occasion to need her help, Ramsey had a feeling that she'd have it should she ask. "She's coming here as well. To dinner I mean. It'll be loud and wonderful. I used to be terrified when they all came together like this. But I finally got over that. It's not something that I can take all the time like the men do. I like to be alone too." Sloan might have at one time, Ramsey thought, but she liked company now. And was good around people.

"Margo is upstairs putting the final touches on the room. Did you want to go ahead and meet her now?" Sloan nodded her head vigorously. As they were going up the long staircase, Ramsey thought of the one in her home, her parents' home.

She'd wanted to slide down the bannister almost as soon as she realized how much fun it would be. But that, like so much of her fun, had been nixed thanks to her sister and brother. She didn't care for either of them very much then, and not any more now. Ramsey wondered if they had wanted to do it, slide down it with their legs around the oak, whether they would have been allowed to do so.

She heard her friend even before they got to the top of the stairs, and Ramsey smiled. Margo was the nicest person you could ever meet. She was also flighty and odd, colorful, and sort of hard to have a conversation with. But she was a brilliant artist, one that Ramsey had admired long before she was as famous as she was now. And Margo owned many of Ramsey's pictures, some of which she'd turned into works of art.

"Oh darlin', have you ever seen such a dwellin' a-fore? Look at all those lovely palates that I can work with." Her over-the-top, fake Southern accent was just bursting with shortened words and phrases. "Why, I could just mosey on down to the orchard behind here and grab me up a couple of them red apples and use them as paints. I'd never be able to match'em up, but there you got it. How are you, Ramsey love? I've missed you again. Have you been taking more of those just lovey pictures? And where is my man, Godan?"

"Fine, Margo, how about you? And Godan is working on something for me. I don't expect to see much of him this trip." She just grinned and looked at Sloan. "This is Mrs. Sloan Emerson. She, along with a few other ladies, is trying to turn this into a prime gallery. You coming here is going to help them. Thank you."

"Oh, pee-shaw. I just love helpin' you out. My, but you sure are a pretty little thing, aren't you? I'd love to paint you sometime. Bright colors are my specialty." Sloan looked at her, and Ramsey shook her head.

When Margo said she wanted to paint you, that's what she wanted to do. She'd have you disrobe, and then as she walked around you while you stood up on a box, she'd smear paint all over your body, then have you roll naked on a canvas so she could finish it. Ramsey had never been a subject of her art, but she knew others who had. Margo would pay you if the art sold, and pay well, but Ramsey liked her privacy more than she did rolling around in paints.

"I just came by to see if you needed anything before we have the preshow in a few days. The people who will be here then will be the ones that have donated money to helping us raise the funds to do this. And then on Saturday, we'll open the doors to the public." Ramsey let the two of them talk and moved to the yard behind the house to make a call. She needed to talk to her dad.

When he answered, she knew that something had happened. Not sure what, but she was sure it had to do with her family. While she and her dad weren't as close as they might have been if things had been better at home, they were beginning to be friendly to each other.

"I've been worried sick about you. Where are you, love? I just need to…I want to see you again. I know that you're really busy with your work and all, but…well, I could use a friendly face and a shoulder to cry on. Please, let me know where you are." Ramsey could see Cash walking down the street with two little kids, a girl and boy, and she could tell even from where she was that he was enjoying their time together more than they were. "Ramsey? Are you there?"

"Dad...I'd like to see you too. But you do know that it's going to upset the rest of them. Mother hates it when I call... what is she going to say if she finds out that you were coming to see me now?" His sudden intake of breath made her smile. "Shocked you, didn't I? But I'm not far from you. Just...please come alone. I won't tell you where I am until you promise me that."

"Anything. I will promise you anything to see you again." She heard his sob and felt horrible about making him jump through hoops to see her. "You've no idea how much I need this. But I'm not at home now. I've had to fly out for a few days. Just tell me when I can come and I'll be there. No matter what, and I won't tell them where I'm going."

"I'm in Sommersville, Ohio." He didn't say anything and she was sure she'd pissed him off for some reason. "I came here to do a favor for someone. Clementine Mantle. You remember her?"

"Yes. I remember.... Ramsey, are you really only a few hours from where we live? Really?" She told him that she was only here for a few more days, then she was going out again. "I'll be there tomorrow. I'm having my flight changed right now. I...I have to sign some paperwork, then I'll be there."

"Good. I...I've changed a great deal since you've seen me." He laughed and she flushed. "And you should be prepared to meet someone that I have...we have a relationship that's just beginning. I've...I have someone in my life now, and I think that I'd like for you to meet him. I think...I hope you'll like him, but if you don't, then that's okay too. I'm not coming home again."

"Honey, I don't even want to go home anymore." She laughed when he did. "I got your package."

Everything in her stilled. Even her heart seemed to stop beating. If he knew, then anyone could know who she was. He was talking, but she couldn't hear him over the buzzing in her head. Finally she sat down on the ground to try to focus.

"Honey, are you all right? Ramsey?" She didn't answer him. "Since you're not denying it, I can assume that I'm right. It took me almost two months to figure out it was you. But the third time the post was brought to me with a local postmark on it, I began to think it was you for some reason, but I was never sure until now. You must have someone send them to me, right? I'm very proud of you, Ramsey. For this and all the other work that you do. I have every cover that you've been on. And I now have a subscription to most of them so I don't miss a single one."

"Does anyone else know?" He told her that he'd never even said it aloud until then. "Dad, I could be killed for those things. Some of the stuff I send you, governments have swept under the rug until you put them in print. You would not believe what I have to do to get them to you. And how many risks that we take even…we have a portable dark room that we print from. That alone could get us killed."

"Christ, Ramsey. Is it…? No. I was going to ask you if you thought it was worth it. But it is, to a lot of people, not just you. I can well imagine what kind of trouble it is to get these to me. Well, I can't, but I'm betting that it's not easy or cheap. You've helped me out, both with my reputation and financially. You've saved a dying newspaper." Ramsey had to think, and she wasn't going to be able to while talking to him. But he seemed to understand that and laughed a little before continuing. "I should be there by tomorrow if things go well here."

"All right. That's good. Dad, just...I'm not R.S. Holms when you get here, remember that. I have to...I'll talk to you tomorrow night. I have a room at the hotel you can use if you want. I'm not staying there right now. It's under my name. Go there, but don't tell anyone who you are. Or who I am. I've not told them as yet." He told her he'd do that and told her that he was looking forward to seeing her. Ramsey hung up before he finished.

Ramsey? Are you all right? Graham touched her mind and she could feel his concern. All she could think about was that her dad knew who she was, but did the others? That was what scared her most of all. If someone came hunting for her and found her with them, what would happen to Graham and the others? *Ramsey?*

My dad, I just spoke to him. He's going to come here to see me tomorrow. I need to...I have to talk to your family about me. About what I've been doing. Do you think that when we have this dinner thing tonight, I could mention it to them then? He told her that would be fine. *They're not going to be happy when they find out everything. You might know who I am, but you don't know the half of it. I've been leading a double life, and the other can get me killed.*

Whatever it is, we can work it out. Hell, I will run away with you if it comes to that. I love you. I will always love you. She wondered how much he'd love her when he found out what she did on the side. *I'll see you at the house at five. I'll let the others know that we should meet earlier and we'll talk then, all right?*

91

Sure. All right then. She wasn't sure of anything right now. As she put her phone back in her pocket, all she could think about was how they were going to be pissed. Godan moved to stand in front of her seconds later, and she stepped back from him involuntarily.

"Missy, you well?" She nodded, but knew that he didn't believe her. "I have news for you. Mr. Dad has been to the warehouse where you have lived. He has men working in it now. It is only a matter of time before he finds what your brother has been doing."

Ramsey had a pretty good idea that her dad knew just what Gregory was up to. And if he didn't, he would soon enough. Gregory and Chad were about to get into some serious shit, and she had been planning this showdown for months. The meth lab that they had there was about to be seriously looked over. And when they were done, a lot of people were going to be arrested, her brother and brother-in-law included.

"He's coming here. My dad." Godan nodded, smiling at her as they walked out of the building and toward the area behind it. "This is not a good thing. He's not going to like what I've become. He'll think I'm a failure."

"You are not failure, Missy. You are a respected person by many. I will show him the error of his ways should he upset you." She smiled at him and walked with him to the edge of the woods that seemed to be in abundance around here. "The others will be close to your mate now. He is having troubles that will not go away, I fear. Those men that are out to get him, do you know them?"

"No, I don't, but I think you're right. Have them make sure that Graham is safe. I think he can fend for himself, but there is no reason for him to be put to the test." Godan said that he would. "Also, when my dad gets here, I want someone to watch over him like they do at his home. I don't want anything to happen to him while he's here."

When her friend walked away, Ramsey moved back into the gallery. Sloan looked like she needed rescuing, and Ramsey thought she'd let her go just a little longer. Being with Margo for more than a few minutes could and would make a grown man cry. Sloan looked close to that now.

"There she is. I have to go." Ramsey covered her smile with a cough when Sloan nearly launched herself at her. "We'll see you tomorrow night, Margo. It was great meeting you."

As they nearly raced out of the door, Sloan was holding onto her like she was going to take her prisoner. As soon as they were across the street in a large open building, Sloan sat down in one of the chairs. A woman that apparently had been prepared for them came with a cup of tea as well as a plate of what looked like scones. The longer Ramsey watched Sloan, the more she realized that Margo had really frazzled her. It was funny, really, to see the rich and very powerful Sloan Emerson like this.

"You know that I love you or you'd never get any of these. Dawn is starting to get wind of the fact that we don't give them out like she thinks we are, but are eating them all by ourselves. I'm going to be stingy from now on." The woman smiled at her when Sloan took the plate. "I'm Jack Emerson. You must be the last mate, Graham's mate, Ramsey."

"I am. But she might need more than what's on the plate. She met Margo just now. I think they're going to be great friends from now on." Sloan told her to shut up and Jack just laughed. "You're the artist, I guess."

"Ad designer. My husband is the mayor. He's coming back tonight from the hearings with the former mayor. I couldn't get away and he had to go alone, poor baby." She shrugged. "I've seen your work. You're very good. I mean, like amazingly good. I'd like to see if we can incorporate some of your pictures into a few designs that I'm working on. The one with the Bengal tigers is the one that I like best of your work."

"You'll have to talk to the mag that printed them. Once I sell them to them, they own the work. But only on the pictures they purchase. I have a few that you can use, so long as my name isn't on them." She asked her why. "I have a contract right now that prohibits me from being in with another ad firm. You can use them, but just not my name until I get out of it. Just a few more months."

Jack nodded and then sat with them. The place was busy, way busier than the firm that she'd been working for. Then she realized who this woman was. Laughing, she asked her if she was ever affiliated with Anderson and Shelling.

"Yes. I worked there for a while, as a matter of fact. You work for them?" She told her indirectly. "I know that they're close to bankruptcy. Are you getting paid?"

"If I don't get paid up front, they don't get the work. And I'm surprised that they'd let you go. Or did they?" Jack just grinned. "The new management is trying to make it work, but I think it's the name rather than the work they're putting out. They would have been better off changing names, but they thought they were buying prestige, and all they got for their money was a big fat lie. The place is good, but not nearly as good as you seem to be."

"Thanks. It was scary there for a while. Luke, my husband, sort of shoved me into this with a bulldozer. I'm glad he did but...." Jack looked at Sloan as she continued. "Nor would I have made it without a little help from my friends."

"I'm sure you would have done it without my help. You're that good." Jack winked at her as Sloan had her third scone and second cup of tea. "You have got to keep me away from Margo, however. That woman is...she can.... Oh dear lord, she's not at all calming, is she?"

They all laughed and Ramsey told them of her first meeting with Margo. "I was just coming out of the ladies' room at this big convention center. I was there for some award; I can't remember why she was there, but she told me she was a painter. I automatically assumed house painter. The way she was dressed — coveralls with so much paint on them — that was a natural assumption I thought. But she took me to see her latest work in progress. There was this man...and wow, what a large man he was, covered in paint from the top of his head to the bottom of his feet. And she walked up to him and painted him. Not the canvas on the floor, but him. And when I say large, I mean a very big, heavy man. As I stood there watching, more stunned than anything, she finished him up then had him rolling on the canvas. She called it *Man with a Bathrobe*. I think she got like forty mill for it."

"Oh dear lord. No wonder you told me not to let her paint me." Sloan shivered. "Thank you so much. I think I owe you big time."

When Sloan was calmed down they moved out to her car

and made their way back to their home. Ramsey had asked to be let off at Graham's house, but Sloan insisted that she come with her. As soon as she was in the house, she knew that she'd been ambushed. Again. Mrs. M was standing there waiting on her.

"Hello, Ramsey. It's been a long time." Ramsey nodded at Clemmie Mantle, but didn't take the hand that was offered. "Still don't trust me, do you? You always were a smart girl. Come. Let's talk, you and I."

~~~

Clemmie loved this child. There were few young people that weren't related to her that she cared all that much for. In fact, a few of her relation she could not stand. But this girl, despite her family, was one of the rare few that she allowed to get close to her.

"I've spoken to your mother recently. Just as nasty as ever. Did you know that your sister and her husband have moved back home?" She said that she did. "And that laze-about brother of yours has as well. Sponging off your father, no doubt."

"I speak to my dad at least once a week. I missed a few here recently, but I spoke to him today." Clemmie knew this of course. He had called her when he found out about her bringing his daughter here. He had sobbed like a child when she told him that she'd been keeping an eye on her. "He's coming here tomorrow. How much do I owe you for having me brought here? I'm sure you had this up your sleeve for a long time."

"What a thing to say to me. And when I spoke to him, he said he was glad that you and he were making amends.

You told him that we have spoken." Ramsey wasn't one for chatter so she nodded. It was another reason for Clemmie to like this girl. "I have some information that I would like for you to pass on to him when he's in the right frame of mind. His son is going to come to harm if he doesn't stop what he's up to now."

"I know. I have people watching him to make sure that nothing comes back on Dad. You are talking about the meth lab in the warehouse, I'm assuming?" Clemmie was impressed. Not many could outdo her when it came to information. "Chad is in deep shit, too. He's got some major gambling debts that are going to take him under soon. Deidra might be a widow before too much longer if I can convince Dad to stop paying Chad's debts off."

Clemmie nodded at her. "She might be better off if that happens. But with her, it's doubtful that she'll learn anything about this. Deidra has a way that makes people believe that she is forever the victim. When in all reality, she's as guilty as can be."

As they sat on the sofa and tea was brought in, Clemmie watched her dismiss the maid and pour the tea herself. Once a lady, always a lady, Clemmie thought. And even though she'd had a harsh upbringing, Ramsey was always a lady. When she took the tea from her, Clemmie sipped quietly, wondering if all the things she had heard about this girl were true. Ramsey had always been very careful to never touch her, so the sad truth was, she knew very little about her. She wondered how much she knew about that too. Clemmie nodded, coming to a decision.

"I'd like to know what you think is going to happen if

you let me see your mind." Ramsey set her cup down but said nothing. "You might not be positive, but you're sure you know something about my abilities. I can tell you that the stories are true. To a point."

"You can read my mind as well as tell some of my future." Clemmie nodded. "Perhaps I don't want to know my future. Or the outcome of some of the things I might do. Knowing is not always good. But the not knowing is wonderful. Freeing, if you want to know the truth of it. It's what I do that scares you, isn't it? I'm assuming that Dad told you who I am for him."

"Yes, he did. I would not have guessed it of you, but I, like him, am very proud of you. But what if I can tell you the outcome of the things going on with your father? I like him, always have, but like you, he's been very careful not to touch me. Addie, my granddaughter, doesn't need to touch you to tell you great things, but I'm old school and need the feeling of warmth to understand what's going to happen." Ramsey asked her if she really thought it was that important. "I don't know why, but I do. I'd very much like to keep you safe, and your father. He's a good man who has made a couple of bad decisions, but I do believe that he's cleaning house, so to speak."

"Is he going to be hurt?" Clemmie told her that she really didn't know. "But you could know, by simply touching me."

"Yes." It was the truth and she could see that Ramsey was weighing all the options of letting her touch her skin. "Your dad really is a good man and deserves better than your mother and siblings. I knew that when I saw the two of you on that deck at your sister's wedding. You told him then, didn't you, how unhappy you were? And then you left."

"I had to." Clemmie told her that she really did. "Had I stayed, I would have said some things that would have hurt more than just him. My family wasn't going to make it easy for me if I hadn't left. And I needed to begin my life, on my terms, and be happy."

They sat there, each of them in their own thoughts. Clemmie had called to Addie to come here now, but she said that she was busy at the moment and would be there soon. She then told Clemmie what was going to happen with Ramsey's family and when.

Her brother is going to be killed before this is done. And while I know the how, I'm not sure that I'll try to change the outcome. He's bad news. She may not get along with them, but she feels that they're her family regardless. But when he is killed, it will drive her mother to hate her more than she does now. Clemmie asked her when this would happen, but Ramsey spoke before she could get an answer.

"If you do this, then you don't hold back. You tell me everything you know or I'll never trust you again." Clemmie nodded but sat very still. "And nothing of my future, please. I don't want you to tell me when I'm going to die or anything like that, okay?"

"Yes. All right. But I want something in return." Ramsey nodded. "When I give you advice, no matter how slim or petty it seems at the time, you will heed it. Promise me that." Ramsey sat there for several more seconds before putting out her hand. Clemmie took it into her warmer ones and nearly fell back at the images that flooded her mind.

The girl had seen so much in the short time she'd been

gone. Done a great many things that might have gotten her killed, too, had she not used her incredible knowledge of the surrounding grounds. Her friends, the white wolves, were also keeping her safe, and Ramsey knew this and kept them as safe as she could. She'd killed, too; a matter of being killed or killing had kept her alive until now. And she'd been reporting things, a great many of them more than just a little dangerous, but deadly as well, using her father's pull and resources to get things out there that normally would have gone unnoticed by the general population.

Clemmie saw the bus and what had happened there. Since Ramsey had touched the children, their stories became hers. The child in the seat behind the driver had killed him. Her parents were being held captive and she was going to free them. But it had been too soon. She'd killed him at the wrong turn on the ride. When Ramsey pulled away, Clemmie looked at her when Ramsey began to tell the rest of the story.

"They were waiting for the bus to come over the next hill. It was a much easier grade and I don't think the bus would have flipped. I don't believe any of them would have died either except the driver." Clemmie asked her how she knew. "We saw them. They were prepared. The police were there, several doctors were on hand. It was done to bring sympathy to the area. They thought that when the media showed there would be an influx of money, fame. It wasn't meant to be a disaster. As it was, families were destroyed, some never to recover. There was money coming in from it, but to help the families and nothing more. It was, right from the start, doomed to fail."

"Yet is was." Ramsey nodded. "How many of the

children lived? How many were you able to save before you were pulled under the fast moving water and down the long waterfall?"

"We were able to get all of them out. No one, not even the driver, was left to go over. Then I finished taking pictures of it all. From the dead driver and the children, to the child that still had the gun cradled against her body when her neck was broken."

"I'm sorry, child." Ramsey didn't say anything to her, and Clemmie wanted to pull her into her arms and simply hold her. But she knew, as surely as she knew the girl's parents, that she'd never been hugged a day in her life until she came to meet Graham and the rest of the Emerson family.

"My dad is coming here. Tomorrow, he said." Clemmie nodded, not reminding her that she'd already told her that once. "I don't think it's going to be a great visit. I have no idea why I think that, but I don't think it's going to go well."

"Your visit with him will go well. Others will be...well, your family is not going to be happy with him. I'm sure that by now, they know that your father cannot be pushed around forever. And that he is a man of his word. They, your family, are going to be in for a very rude awakening." Ramsey smiled. "Yes, I knew you'd like that. But you'll be fine and the visit will be great. Trust me on that."

CHAPTER 6

"I don't understand what you're telling me. Run it again." Krista smiled tightly at her luncheon friends. "You must have done something wrong in running it. Do it again."

"I have, madam. Several times. It says that it is declined. Perhaps you should notify your bank of the situation." Krista snatched the card from him and stuffed it in her purse. Of all the.... The man cleared his throat at her and she looked up at him. "The check, madam. You will still need to pay the check. And at this point, we will require cash only."

She had no cash. Not even a dime to make a call, if it even cost that much anymore. She had no clue if there were even pay phones about. Looking around the table, she wanted to tell them that this was all a mistake, but deep inside of her, she knew that it wasn't. Ram had done just what he'd said he would do.

"Just put it on mine. You can owe me, Krista." Caroline smiled at her...not a friendly smile, but one that said you are so fodder for the gossip mill when I leave here. "It more than likely a mistake at the bank, and you'll be able to clear it up shortly."

Thanking her, Krista thought of all the things she was

going to say to her husband when she saw him again. The nerve of him cutting her off like this. As she left the restaurant she wished now that she'd paid more attention to his lecture yesterday about spending and limits. Surely, she had thought, he wasn't talking about her.

He'd cut them off, he told them all at his grand meeting, and there would be no more indiscriminate outpouring of his money. Deidra and Chad had been there, as well as Gregory. She had been late to the meeting he'd called, and had thought, hoped really, that it would have been over by the time she'd gotten there. But he'd waited, saying that it was important that they all know what he'd done.

"There will be a limit on your spending for each day. I thought about making it weekly, but then I wasn't sure on what day to start and finish it, so daily works just as well. After you hit your limit for the day, then you will not be able to charge anything, not even a newspaper, on the card that I will give you at the end of this meeting. There will not be any cash advances either, from me or the banks. As of now, what you have in your pockets will be all you get from me and this estate." Deidra asked him if that meant her too. "It means all of you."

Krista thought at the time it was a grand idea. She could hold it over their heads when they came to her for cash, and Ram would never know. Krista was thinking of all the ways she could get more from her family when Ram turned to her.

"You, too, will be set on limits. You will follow the same rules that the children are. No more buying dresses you'll never wear, no more luncheons where you buy everyone's meal, and you will no longer be able to have your hair done

104

weekly. No one needs that much primping, I don't care who you are."

"You can't be serious, Ram." She laughed a little, thinking it was a show for the children. "I suppose you and I will talk about this later."

"No. We're talking now. So if you have any questions I'll listen to them, but there will be no changing my mind. We might be well off, but the way you three are going through money, we won't be for long. I have made up a contract for each of you. It outlines the amount you will get daily and what happens if you happen to spend less. I don't foresee that ever becoming an issue, but should there be a time, then that money will roll over into the next day, and then the next until you spend it. But at the end of the week, all monies left will return to me." Krista just smiled at him. Even then with his hard tactics, she knew that he would never do this to her, his wife. "Also, Gregory, you have two months to get a job and move out. You're nearly thirty-five years old, and there is no reason that I should be supporting you. If at the end of that time you don't have a job, rent will be taken from your allowance weekly. I'm not kidding about this."

"He's been trying to find something. There are not a lot of jobs out there for the things he can do." Ram asked her what things it was he could do, and for the life of her she could only think of him being her son. "I don't know what has brought this on, Ram, but I do not care for your tone. I want you to make things like they were before. The children, our children, have gotten used to a better lifestyle than this, and you cannot mean to take that from them at this time in their lives. They're stressed enough as it is."

"Tough. And it's not just our children that are going to abide by these rules, Krista. You are included as well." She was so shocked by his tone that when he turned to Deidra, all Krista could think about was he had lost his mind. As he continued on his tirade, she thought of all the things she could do to him and not one thing came to mind. "Deidra, you and Chad have one month as well to find you a place to live and a job. I don't care which one of you is working, but you will find employment or I will cut you both off. No more allowances and no more credit. As of now, you are on probation. One month."

"Oh, Daddy, don't be silly. I'm your little princess. You can't seriously be thinking I should flip hamburgers for the rest of my life. That's just not going happen. I'm not suited for menial labor. I've just had my nails done." When she fluttered her eyes at her daddy, Krista wanted to get up and slap her. She'd never had the urge to hit her daughter before, but at this moment, the feeling took her breath away. "What would you do with yourself if we were to move out? Not to mention, who will help you in your golden years? You can't have that many years left. Besides, Chad and I love it here, being with you and Mommy. I know that you like having us here."

"No, I have grown quite tired of having you here. You're old enough to stand up on your own, both of you. You've been married to him...." Ram pointed to Chad like he knew something he wasn't happy with as he continued. "For nearly ten years, and I have supported you every month while the two of you were getting deeper and deeper in debt. It's time you got out of my home and found your own way in life. I will not support you any longer. And as for my golden years?

I've taken care of that on my own. Depending on any of you to do so would not be good, I'm thinking."

He handed them each a file. Krista wasn't going to open hers, she had sat there with it on her lap trying her best to think of a way to change his mind about this. She had no idea at that time what her spending limits were going to be, but surely he didn't expect her to watch her money as if she were a pauper.

"This is a record of the spending you each had over the last thirty days. Each of you, and I do mean each of you, have gone well beyond what could be considered lavish spending." He picked up a sheet of paper before reading from it. "Deidra, you spent nearly eleven thousand dollars on clothing. Where on earth would you wear such a grand amount of clothing?"

"It was only for two dresses. I have to look good when we go out. I am Chad's wife." He huffed at her. "You're just very lucky, Daddy, that they didn't have the third dress I wanted in my size. It was a good deal more than both of the ones that I bought." She giggled and he glared.

"Chad. Your spending is outrageous. Why do you have a charge on here for fourteen thousand dollars at the country club? I had no idea you even went there. You, as far as I know, don't golf or swim."

"There was a bachelor party and they said that I had to pay for the damages. I don't think I did it, but when the bill came.... Listen old man, what does it matter what any of us spend? It's not like you don't have the funds to cover it. We're family, after all." Chad grinned at Krista with a wink before he looked at Ram again. "This is a very nice show of your power, and we can all try to cut back, but this meeting is taking up a lot of my time and I have to get going."

"Sit down." Krista had never heard Ram raise his voice before, and realized then that he was mad. Very much so. "This is not just a meeting. This is the way that things are going to be from now on. You will either abide by my rules or you will find yourself out on the curb."

He'd said that to her the other day, something about him liking his peace and quiet. Well, if he thought it was noisy before, it was about to get ten times worse. Before she could make any sort of threat in that area, he turned to Gregory.

"No more, Gregory. I will not pay for your drugs, I won't pay for any more rehab, nor will I be responsible for any of your mishaps. The lab that you have set up in the warehouse is gone as well. And if you're smart, which I don't think you are, you'll stay away from that area until they've finished their investigation. You are on your own when it comes to your other life, and I want no part of it. There will be help should you need or want it, but if you leave the center this time, I will wash my hands of you completely. And if you think I'm fucking with you, try me." Gregory stood up and Krista did as well. No one was going to hurt her baby boy. Not even her own husband. "You will find a job, get dried out, or we're finished."

"I hate you. I have always hated you. And if you think this ends here, then you're stupider than this fucking contract is." Gregory tossed the papers back in his face and left the room. Ram just stared after him as the door slammed.

"I will not listen to you telling me what I have spent money on. I have supported you for decades, Ramsey Stockholm, and I will spend our money as I see fit." He only smiled at her. "You'll not do this to me, or so help me, you're going to regret it."

"The only thing I regret, Krista, is the way I treated our daughter, Ramsey." She felt as if he'd slapped her.

The new credit cards had been handed out. They were a plain bank issued card, unlike the one she'd had made with a picture of Deidra and Chad on their wedding day. Then he'd given them their contracts. She was only allotted one hundred dollars per day to spend. Surely there had to have been a mistake.

But she hadn't asked him about it, determined not to ever speak to him again. And now here she was, in a restaurant with her friends and as broke as the homeless man down the street. Leaving the country club—her haven, as she'd once thought of it—she made her way to the house while trying to contact Ram. He was going to fix this or...or something would happen. She had no idea what, but she'd make him pay.

Each time she called him, it went straight to voice mail. Not leaving a message the first few times, she knew that he was avoiding her. And her anger. But after the fifth time of getting the same recording of him being unavailable, she finally let go.

"You miserable piece of horse shit. You did this to me so that I'd be embarrassed. Well, you messed up then, didn't you? Now the entire country club knows that you're broke. Broke. Ha. And you are going to make it so that things are the way they were before, or so help me I will hunt you down and murder you. Do you hear me, Ram? I will fucking kill you."

Going to her room, she thought of what she'd said. It more than likely wasn't a good idea to have said those things to her husband, especially with it being recorded, but she was mad. Spitting mad, as a matter of fact. When her maid didn't come to her right away, she rang for her again just as the phone next to her bed rang. Thinking it was Ram, she only picked it up and waited for his apology.

"Madam, this is Kent, the butler to the household. Your maid has been let go as of this morning. I do believe that it was a part of your contract to give up on certain pleasantries concerning the staff." She wanted to scream at him to get her back, but he continued before she could say a word. "And Mr. Stockholm is on a trip and will return in a month. Is there anything I can do for you at the moment?"

Krista slammed the phone down. There was plenty she was going to do for Ram when she found him. And he'd better know that he shouldn't fuck with her like this and think to get away with it.

~~~

Ram was terrified. He'd not seen Ramsey in almost ten years, and in all that time, he'd thought of their meeting like this every day. Not quite this many years had passed in his dreams of having his daughter home again, but he still thought about her. Every hour of every day. When the plane landed, taxied down the runway, all he could think about was he was going to mess this up. He didn't know how, but he knew that she was going to tell him thanks but no thanks when he told her what he needed…wanted from her.

As soon as he was in the smallish building that was the hub of the town she was in, he looked around for her. All he had in his head was the beautiful young woman that he'd seen that fateful night. Ram only hoped that she was there and some spark of recognition would make them connect. Then he saw her.

Ram had a few moments to just stare at her. Christ, he'd thought her beautiful before, but she nearly glowed with it now. Her hair, a dark color all those years ago, was now streaked from the sun. Her face, a face of a goddess, was browned by the same sun, and not a tanning booth as her sister used. She was taller than he remembered, maybe slightly thinner, but she was his little girl. When she threw back her head in laughter with the man that stood beside her, Ram felt his heart twist at all he'd missed, and then she looked right at him.

He wasn't sure what to do when she came to him. Hug her? Shake her hand? It had been too long, even longer if he counted the first years of her life, since he'd done anything more than ignore her. He hurt for that as well.

"Hello, Dad."

Overwhelmed with the need to touch her, he pulled her to him and hugged her tightly. It felt wonderful, and when she wrapped her arms around him and hugged him back, Ram started to sob like a little boy. She couldn't hate him and hug him like she had.

He held her tightly for longer than he knew was proper. But his heart was aching so badly that he knew that if he let her go, even for a moment, she'd be gone again and he'd be left alone. When she pulled back but didn't leave him, he felt like a man atop the world.

"Dad, I'd like you to meet Graham Emerson. Graham, this is my dad, Ram Stockholm." The boy, man really, smiled at him, and he knew in that moment that he loved his little girl.

111

"We're going to be staying at his house while you're here."

"All right." He turned to get his luggage and saw that a large man had them in his hands. The man bowed at the waist at him and Ram nodded back. He had no idea who this man was, but he had the distinct feeling that he'd kill him if he made the wrong move. Turning back to Ramsey, he spoke to her and Graham.

"I wasn't sure what kind of reception I'd have." He was babbling and couldn't seem to stop it. "I've been such a fool for all these years, and now I just don't know what to do with myself."

"The grand opening to the gallery is in a few days, so I hoped that you'd like to go to that. Mostly just finger food and people walking around acting like they know what they're doing." Ram nodded at Graham, grateful for the conversation he was making to cover for him. "Then the next night, the real opening is the big deal. If you didn't bring your tux, we have someone here that can fit you out in one. Sloan, my sister-in-law, said that every man should have a tux even if he only wears it to his own funeral."

"Ramsey told me about it, so I'm fixed up." Graham nodded and led them to a long sleek limo. "Nice. Very nice. I don't want you to be offended, young man, but I've done some checking on you. You and your family are not just well thought of, but seem to have it going very well for you."

"We do. I have a doctorate in marine biology. I've been working on the lakes and rivers in Ohio since I've been here. There are a great many things that we can do to fix what we have. And I'd like to be a part of getting things back to the way they were hundreds of years ago. Clean waterways and streams." Ram nodded and glanced at his daughter. She was being very quiet, and he was beginning to worry. When she walked away to answer her phone, he looked at Graham. "It's not you. She doesn't say much."

"Why not?" Graham said he didn't know, but he didn't babble much either unless he was nervous. "Are you? Nervous, I mean?"

"Yes, sir." Ram told him he was as well. "Ramsey and I were going to tell you when we get to our house, but I wanted to have a few minutes alone with you to explain something. I mean, it's not that important that you know, but I'd feel better if you did."

"You're not human." Graham nodded but didn't look surprised that he knew. "I have my own way of looking into things. And I had a long talk with Clemmie Mantle. She's a woman who says what she thinks and damn how you feel about it afterwards. I understand that you know her too."

"She's the grandmother to one of my sisters-in-law, Addie Emerson." Ram knew this as well. "You're going to meet them all tonight. Sloan is having a nice get together with all of us so you can be overwhelmed all at one time instead of over the time you're here. But we're not too bad of a family." Ram nodded and looked at Ramsey, who was still on the phone. Mostly, he could see now, listening.

"I've missed her. Not just since she left us, but before that. I was a shitty father." Graham said nothing and Ram laughed. "You're not going to tell me I'm wrong, are you?"

"I'm not going to come between you and Ramsey, and I think it's wonderful that the two of you are making time to see each other. But...." He closed the trunk to the limo when

113

everything was loaded in and turned to him. "But if you hurt her, upset her beyond reason, I will tear your throat out without a second's hesitation. That you can take to the bank and count on it. She's my life, and I won't have you hurting her any more than is just normal stuff."

Ram believed him too. When Ramsey came back to join them, she didn't say anything but climbed into the big car after he did. Graham leaned his head in and kissed Ramsey and said he'd see her later. Then they were off. Apparently the younger man had an appointment that could not be missed, Ramsey told him.

"He loves you." Ramsey, sitting across from him, nodded. "You love him? I mean, I don't know what love looks like on you, but I'd say you do."

"I think I do. He's a good man. Takes care of me." Ram nodded, not sure what to say now. "I'm glad you're here, Dad. Really I am. But I'll be honest with you when I tell you I'm not sure what to do. We were never what you could call close, and while I love you, I'm not sure what you want from being with me."

He let out a long breath. "Me either. I mean…we hardly know each other anymore, like you said. And as much as I hate to admit it, I didn't know you before you left either. But I've been keeping up with you. Me and Kent, we have this big map where we pinpoint your movements. You've been about everywhere, haven't you? And those pictures? I think I have every one of them stored away."

"I love what I do." He nodded, and told her he could see that in her work. "Taking the perfect shot, getting what I want from the animals that I put on film, it's the greatest thing I could do. Some of those animals haven't ever been seen before."

"Some of those shots, I'll have to admit, scared the snot out of me. Those tigers you shot in Africa looked like you were right in the den with them. And those snakes." Ram shivered. "Never been one to be around snakes when they just show up. Can't think of going into a pit of them just to take a few pictures."

"I took rolls and rolls of film. I use a digital camera too, but I love the film and developing it on my own. It's like a gift that I can open that no one has ever seen before." He could see the joy on her face and felt it wrap around him. "If you're here for a little while, I'll show them to you if you want. I have them all over the room that I use for an office right now. Graham and I have talked about converting the old barn to a studio that I can use when I'm there with him."

"I'll be here for as long as you let me." And he knew that was true too. He'd only planned to stay a week, two at the most, but hoped for a month. But now that he was here, he never wanted to leave. Never set foot in his cold angry house again.

He watched her as she leaned back on the seat and closed her eyes. Graham said that she didn't say much, but he'd bet that when she did, it was important. Ram supposed that being out working her job the way she did would require her to be quiet. He thought of the man that had put his luggage in the trunk and started to ask her about him. But his phone rang again and he smiled at the caller ID.

"Mom?" He told her it was. "She's probably not happy that you've come to see me. She never cared all that much for me."

"She doesn't know where I am. I had a thought to tell her when I spoke to her last, but I didn't want her intruding. And after the way I left them, all pissed off and all, I knew that they'd be beating down my door to demand that I make things right for them." He had expected Ramsey to ask him what he'd done, but she only nodded. She more than likely thought it was none of her business, when it actually was. Simply because she was his daughter.

They pulled up in front of a beautiful home a few minutes later. Ram could see that the house, while new, had a look and feel to it that made one think that generations of Emersons had lived there. The lawn was well maintained, and the wraparound porch was inviting and warm looking. He felt like he'd come home, a feeling he'd never felt in his own home before.

"It's lovely." She looked up at the house and smiled. "You like it here? I mean, a stationary home for a change?"

"The bed has been something to get used to. I'm still spending about half the night on the floor. But Graham understands. I've been in the woods in some form or another for a long time." She turned to him and smiled. "But I do like it here. It's really pretty, and the others…Godan and the others can run where they want."

"And they are? I'm assuming that they're wolves like Graham." Ramsey stared at him for several seconds before she nodded. "And they take care of you? Keep you safe while you're out doing your job?"

"They do. We keep each other safe." When the man came out of the house, he leaned in and whispered to Ramsey. As he carried the bags inside, Ram looked at her. "Godan wants to get your scent, as the others do. He wants to make sure that you're safe while you're here. And so are they. You won't harm them, will you, Dad?"

"No. Never." As he made his way up the few stairs to the porch, he thought about her not including herself in her request. He supposed that the way he'd treated her as a child, she could expect that he would harm her. Well, Ram thought, not so long as he had a breath in his body would any harm come to his child again. Verbally or physically.

Chapter 7

Graham was sitting in his office when the door opened with a loud bang. Before he could rise up to see what the hell was going on, he was tossed to the top of his desk and cuffs put on his wrists. He felt his wolf move along his skin, but he knew that if he shifted now, he'd be dead before his first breath as a wolf.

"Graham Emerson, you're under arrest for the murder of Alison and Peter Anderson. You have the right to remain...."

Graham reached for Hunter while the man read him his rights. *I'm being arrested for the murder of those two people. I don't know where they're taking me, but keep Ramsey safe for me.* Hunter said he was just about to his house, but he'd be there before they got him taken away. *I'll need a lawyer. And as much as I love Luke, I think this is something that needs to not be a family affair.*

I agree. I'm talking to Sloan too. She's calling Shawn again. Lucky for us he was here for the opening. I can see them now. We're in the parking lot of your office. Christ, I'm glad that you decided to have one there on your property too.

Graham was jerked up from the desk and then nearly

thrown to the floor when his feet tangled with one of the men in the room. Guns were drawn and they were all pointing at him. Graham felt Ramsey touch his mind just as they exited his office building.

What the hell is happening? He told her what he knew. *Dad and I are close. I'll be there in a few minutes. What the hell are they talking about? Do you even know? Please tell me this is not about those deaths again.*

Yes, it is. As you know, I found the body of a woman about a month and a half ago. She'd been bludgeoned to death by blows to the head, and then tied to something and dumped in the river. When the thaw came, she floated to the top and got wrapped up in a barge I was cleaning up. Then about three weeks ago, I found the body of a male in the fields behind my brother's land. He watched as Hunter was talking to the man who seemed to be in charge. *I didn't do this. You have to believe me.*

Of course you didn't do this. It's just stupid that they think you could. I'm nearly there. Dad is calling a couple of his attorneys in as well. He told her that was good. *I'm not sure what they think they have on you, but we can get this straightened out. All right?*

Yes. Graham was shoved into the back of the cruiser, and thought that he should have been paying more attention. *I'm going to jail. I don't know where, but I'm in the car now.*

The door was suddenly opened after the man had just shut it, and he was pulled from the car and into her arms. He couldn't hold onto Ramsey, but he was glad that she was there. He looked at the man that was laying on the ground next to the car, and then at Ramsey.

"He pissed me off." Graham nodded and kissed her. When he lifted his head, she was crying. "I don't know what to do. I have been…I don't have a clue how to save you from this."

"I don't either." Which was true. He didn't know why they thought he'd done this heinous crime or why the couple was dead. Up until yesterday, he'd not even known what their names had been. This time when he was shoved in the cruiser it was done with a gentler hand. He had no idea which one of the pissed off men had said something—both Hunter and Ram looked like they might have—but he was grateful for it.

The men driving the car didn't talk. Graham had never been in the back of a cruiser before, not even as a kid when they'd gone to the station as a class trip. Perhaps they didn't talk like they did on the television. He was terrified though, more afraid than he'd ever been in his life.

Godan and the other pack are going to the area where Hunter said you found the bodies. He'll find something. He's born to track. Hunter and Sloan are talking with Shawn and Dad. Dad is saying that whatever the cost, we'll have you out on bail if there is one. Graham asked her if she thought there would be. *No. To be honest, I don't think they'll set one for you. You're wealthy, have your own plane, and you have the support of an entire town at your call. They'd be stupid to let you out on bail.*

That's not really what I wanted to hear. He had to smile at her huffing at him. *I guess I should be grateful that they didn't shoot first and ask me questions when it was too late.*

I'm not entirely sure why they didn't. I mean, they have a real hard-on about you going down for these crimes. Makes me wonder if they don't have some other agenda than just bringing you in for the murders. He'd never thought of that, and said as much to Ramsey. *I've done this sort of thing before. Not with someone I*

121

know, but I have investigated a few incidents where the innocent are just that, but are found guilty by the law to make the crime go away. But this isn't local.

No. I'm betting Max — he's the sheriff — I'm betting he has no idea what's going on. Had he known, I would have had plenty of time to get my shit together or simply run until I could figure this out. Graham felt better just talking to her about this. None of it seemed to be in his favor, but he felt calmer by talking to her. *I wonder what sort of evidence they have that points to me. I mean, whatever it is, it can't be right. I don't know those people.*

You leave that to me. He was almost afraid to ask her what she was going to do. *And if you see me in the cell next to you, don't be surprised. I think this is going to call for some of my more quiet moves. But if I get caught, I might be arrested too.*

Don't get yourself hurt. She assured him that she wouldn't dream of it. *Why do I not feel reassured by that statement?*

I'm going to see what I can find out. In the meantime, don't say a word to anyone. Not even to ask for a glass of water. Don't drink anything, don't touch anything. Your lawyer is on his way, and he will do all the talking. Shawn will be there when you get there. He asked her where she was going to be. *Looking into the deaths of Alison and Peter Anderson. Someone had to have killed them, and I want to know who and why.*

Graham felt better. Not completely, but better than he had when they arrested him. Leaning back against the seat, he thought of all the things he was going to do to Ramsey when he got out of there. First and foremost, he was going to marry her. Then, if she wanted, have about ten or so children.

~~~

It only took her one call to find out who the couple were.

Alison Mitchell was the daughter of a prominent lawyer and business owner. And surprise, surprise, she'd had a falling out with her father just before she had left home to live with Peter Anderson. She'd been sixteen and him twenty-five.

"They have a child." The paper was laid in front of her, and she looked up at Godan. "I cannot find a record of his death, so he is out there somewhere. Should I find him?"

"Yes. But take one of the Emerson men with you. I don't know what sort of shit is going on with this, but it might help." Godan nodded and moved to the door before stopping again. "You will be safe, won't you?"

"I am, without fail, always striving to be safe, my lady." Smiling at him as he left her to work, she thought of all the times they had come very close to being killed. Not just the bus—that had been bad enough—but a couple of times he'd saved her from being eaten by some wild beast that had been a little pissed at her for being in his domain.

The plate that was suddenly in front of her had her looking up. It took her several seconds to focus on the man standing there and to remember who he was. Cash Emerson had been moving in and out of her life for the past several weeks. Mostly it was to flirt—the man was really good at it—but there were times, like right now, that he was seeing to her, as he called it.

"Eat that." Nodding, she picked up the sandwich, just realizing how hungry she was. "And if you leave a crumb on that plate, I'm going to call in the troops. Mable made that just for you, and I won't have her insulted when you're too busy to eat."

"I forget to eat sometimes." He nodded, and she had a

feeling that he did understand what she was talking about. "I have to find a board to hang up. Something that I can use as a flow chart."

"I can get you that. Tell me what you need. I have to do something, and I have no idea what them people at Hunter's house are about. Lawyers. Sometimes I think we only need them 'cause they said we do." Ramsey could see that he was worried. So was she, but she was at least working and he wasn't.

"I have some information on the couple. It's not good, not any of it." She handed him a thick file when he sat down across from her. "The father of Alison, Samuel Mitchell, had an arrest warrant out for Anderson. He claimed that he kidnapped his daughter and then raped her. Not true so far as I can see. She was genuinely in love with him and him her. There might be a child. Godan is looking into that for us."

"That Godan, he and the rest of them, they're all snow wolves, aren't they?" Ramsey told him that they were. "Rare, did you know that? I'm sure you did, but I was wondering how rare you think they are."

"I think that Godan and his family are the last of them. At one time I think they were called the Melville Island wolves. But since there are so few of them, I don't think many know that." Cash nodded but said nothing. "What is it you're trying your best not to ask?"

"Graham said you saved them. That this man's wife and child were murdered and that you tried to save them too. Because of their coat, right?" Ramsey nodded, not sure where he was going. "They bit you? Those wolves, they bite you to have a link?"

"Yes." He nodded again. "What is it? I told Graham that it happened. He said that he didn't see a problem with it."

"No. No problem. But I'm thinking that if you convert, and I'm thinking that you will, you might have a bit of them in you. Their gene, it's pretty strong. I'm thinking that if you aren't a white wolf when you shift, then you'll be mostly that. It's been a while since I read up on my lore, but you've been their alpha for a long while, changing blood with them when the need came up. You might be about as close to being one of them as you can be." Ramsey looked at the mark on her wrist. Godan's wife had done that to her just before she'd died. "You're marked by them."

"She was dying." Cash nodded. "I didn't mean to hurt her, but when I tried to lift her off the board she'd been tied to, she snapped at me and tore into my skin."

"Might be that I'm wrong. Been that a couple of times in my life. Not that I like to brag or nothing, but I'm a learned man." She grinned when he winked at her. "I'm going to go do some shopping for equipment for us. You need anything else besides one of them boards?"

After she wrote out a quick list, Cash left her to her work. There wasn't a lot of information to go on, but she dug through it all. Calling in a couple of favors had the fax machine behind her singing out a grinding tune just as Cash returned with Godan.

The board, a wipe off kind that she liked, was set up. Mable came by about an hour later and started in on the kitchen to cook for them. Graham had a cook, but it was her days off and they'd been fending for themselves. Shawn and Luke took over the living room, and the rest of his brothers,

125

all three of them, walked between the two areas answering questions, getting things they needed, and keeping them informed. Ramsey was looking at a file when Clemmie and Addie came in and sat down.

"You know that we can't do this for you, don't you?" Ramsey nodded at Clemmie, not sure what she was getting at. As far as she knew, they hadn't been helping at all. Not that it mattered, there were almost too many helping as it was. "But you're on the right track with the paper you have in your hand." She looked at the birth certificate in her hand and wondered how the hell that was going to be helpful. So far as she could see, Peter had taken a minor to his bed.

Clemmie left and Addie grinned at her. "My grandmother wants so badly to tell you where to find the information that you need. But we have learned that if you can't explain how you come to have the information, then it would do you little to no good to have it as proof."

"Is it a trait of your family to talk in riddles?" Addie laughed again when a little boy came in and sat on her lap. Him sitting on Addie's lap brought back so many memories that she started to tell one that she thought of when she was alone sometimes. "I saw this little guy once when I was out working. He was about five or so. He and his family were foraging for food. There wasn't a lot to find…the river that they'd been using had been dried up for years. But they looked, and would usually find something to fill their bellies, if only for a single day. But the kid was digging with a stick on the rims of what had once been a deep flowing river when suddenly he cried out. A large snapping turtle had buried himself down under the dirt during the hottest part of the day, and he'd come upon his resting place."

"What happened to him? Did the turtle eat his legs off?" Ramsey smiled at the little boy, who she thought was named Kelly. "I bet there was all kinds of blood everywhere."

"No. No blood." Kelly actually looked disappointed. "But he did pull the turtle out of the dirt by his tail. He was as big as the little boy was, and more than likely weighed more than this kid did as well. I have a picture here if you want to see it."

She moved to the file she needed and pulled up the pictures of the turtle and the family. Kelly came to her side of the desk and crawled up in her lap. Ramsey moved him to a better position so that she could tell him the story as she moved through the pictures.

"Meat is something that they don't get a lot of, much less other things they can eat, and him finding this was going to make his family the envy of all the other men and women around them. His dad helped the young boy pull the meat to the big fire, and they worked for hours on cutting it up. The mother dried as much of it as she could and stored it in the pottery jars that she had traded things for in the other village." Kelly had her pause where the father and son were cooking the meat over an open flame. Ramsey waited until he had his fill of the picture before she moved on. "Most of the time when something of value is found like this, some of the others will gang up on the one with it and take it from him, sometimes killing his family in the process. But these people thought it such a good omen that such a grand thing had been given to them that they helped the family with the turtle, and were rewarded for their effort with some of it for their own families."

The last picture was of the little boy. He was wearing the chest plate of the turtle around his neck, and a large claw was on a long piece of string that hung from his wrist. Kelley pulled up her sleeve and fingered the matching one on her wrist. There were about a dozen such things on string or leather around her arm, but Kelly only looked at the turtle one.

"He is very lucky to have his mom and dad." Ramsey looked at Addie when Kelly spoke. She shook her head and Ramsey understood it to mean that it was okay for him to talk about them. "I have Jack and Luke as my parents, and a whole bunch of aunts and uncles too. They took me to their hearts, Grandda Cash said to me the other day, and that makes me very special."

"Yes. You're very lucky that someone loves you enough to make you a part of their family. I have that too. That's why I have these bracelets around my wrist like this. They show people that I visit that I'm a part of a tribe somewhere. Or in my case, a lot of tribes." He nodded and then pulled her sleeve back down. "Kelly, the next time I go to see some of the people that I film, I'm going to tell him all about you and Hannah and the rest of my family."

"Maybe someday I can go there too, and I can tell him myself." Ramsey only nodded, knowing that would never happen.

When Kelly left them, Addie thanked her. She asked her for what. "For not telling him that they are all dead. That a tsunami came in the following month and washed not just the people away, but the entire village as well. Thank you for giving him a story that was nice and not harsh like you knew it to be." Ramsey flushed. "You're a good person, Ramsey Emerson. And I'm glad that you're a part of this family."

Sloan joined them a little while later, along with Jack and Dawn. And while Ramsey was used to it being silent—not just quiet, but silent—when she was working, the chatter of the woman didn't bother her as much as it might have. When Kimber Emerson came into the room a little before five, she reminded them that there was a party to attend and they'd better get their butts in gear. Ramsey didn't move from her seat.

"I'm not going. That was the deal." Jack crossed her arms over her chest and Sloan started tapping her foot. "You can look all pissy as much as you want, but I don't do these things. I am not a person that stands in front of the camera, I'm the one behind it."

"And that's your cover." She asked Dawn what she meant. "You're going to be the photographer for the event. No one will give you a second glance, and you'll get to be there with us. Hurry up, I've brought you a dress."

"Dress?" They all nodded and she shook her head. "I don't do dresses either. I haven't had one on since…well, since my sister got married, ten years ago."

"Then you'd better hurry. We might have to show you a thing or two about dressing up." Ramsey started to protest again but Sloan continued. "Graham is going to be there. Your dad got him bail. He was going to surprise you, but I think it's important that you get there, so I had permission to tell you. Surprise."

Graham was out on bail? She jumped up from the desk and made her way around it. The paper she'd been looking at when Kelly came in floated to the floor. As she bent to pick it up, something caught her eye. The numbers that claimed the date of birth for Alison were different. A smaller font, and they didn't line up with the other things on the line. Someone had doctored the birth certificate. And the only person who could have done that was her father. He did this.

"Are you coming?" She nodded at Dawn but stared at the paper. How many people were involved in this? Why was Graham being targeted as the murderer of people he didn't know? And one thing about Allison's father kept bothering her. He was a business owner of several very high end businesses and a single tire shop. The kind where people with very little funds could buy a used tire and have it mounted. It was low profit and high maintenance too. Laying the paper down, knowing that it would do her no good to try and figure it out, she followed the women out of the room.

She was standing in the shower when she felt something touch her mind. It wasn't Graham, but it was someone she knew. The touch was faint but lingering, and before she could ask who was there, one of the pack spoke to her.

It is I, Mike. We have found something that you should see. Not now, but at first light. She told him that she'd come now. *No, Missy. Too dangerous. Men are about that should not be here. We have camera set up for you as you said.*

Can they see you? He told her that they could not. *Don't approach them, none of you. I can't have you getting hurt. I need you.*

And we you, Missy. Master Graham, he did not do this thing. We know that. She said she knew that as well. *What we have found will make him clear of it. For all time. And the cameras will show rest.*

As she was pulling on the dress, and what a dress it was, she asked Godan to make sure that the pack was safe on their land. He said that he would, but that two at a time were watching the area that he'd been to.

We have found gun. It is hidden in big tree, but we found it for you. Nearly weak with relief, she told him that she was thankful for his help. *We will come to big house tonight. There is trouble brewing there too. Miss Clemmie, she said to call her, she told us that big woman is coming and you would need us to keep you from killing her.*

Ramsey had an idea who it might be but didn't ask. Pulling her hair up into a ponytail then coiling it all round her head, she reached out to Graham and told him what they'd found for him.

Godan is with me. He won't leave my side. Something about a big woman coming. She told him it was more than likely her mother. *Is she a big woman?*

No, but that's what they call people with a big mouth. I'm guessing that Godan thinks she's going to be unhappy when she gets here. Graham laughed. *I forgot about this thing tonight. I'm going to be the camera man for it, I guess. But I'm so glad that you're going to be there too. I've missed you so much.*

So long as later you and I can find a dark corner and I can show you how much I appreciate what you've found. I'm thinking it might take a while, so you should get as many pictures as possible taken right away before I ravage you. Ramsey stood in front of the mirror and thought about him finding her. Reaching up under her dress, she pulled the tiny little panties off and tossed them on the bed.

131

When you find that corner, know that I'm completely naked beneath this dress. Not even a pair of panties are going to keep you from your appreciation. His moan in her head had her holding onto the wall. She was wet, soaking wet, and could not wait to find him.

Making her way down the stairs after cleaning up again, she noticed her dad standing there waiting for her. Everyone else, it seemed, had gone on ahead. He told her that her things were already in the limo and that he was going to escort her.

"Mother is on her way, did you know that?" He nodded, and looked so sad that she wanted to hit her mother for doing this to him. "I'm not worried about her if you're thinking that. I've been making it on my own for a long time now, and her opinion doesn't matter to me. It shouldn't matter to you either. She is nothing to us anymore."

"Regardless, she will still be an embarrassment when she finds that I've come here to see you. Not that I care, but this thing with the Emerson's is going to be in the middle of it should she decide that she isn't going to take this laying down. And I do have to warn you about some of the things I did to them before I left, and she's going to be madder than a wet hornet. I did some things to her…well, to them all before I left there." He explained what he'd done and she had to laugh. "You won't think it's so funny when she comes here and ruins this night for you and the others."

"She can try, Dad. If I were you, I'd not worry about her either. She might just be in for a big surprise when she messes with my family." Her dad stared at her for several seconds before he laughed. "Mom is going to be in for a major awakening if she fucks with me now. I'm not that little girl she slapped at Deidra's wedding."

"I cannot wait. No sir, I cannot wait now." He grinned at her before speaking again. "I might even have to learn how to use one of those cameras so I can look at this again and again. She is going to have a brick."

Ramsey knew a little more about her mother than she thought her dad might know. And if she messed with her too much, Ramsey was going to put her in her place. She had long since gotten over being the last man out. Ramsey Stockholm Emerson was a woman with power now.

Chapter 8

Graham had to look twice when she came into the room. Had he been with her at the house, he would still have had trouble believing that this woman was his mate. Christ, she looked good enough to eat. And he so wanted to feast on her.

Walking to her, he watched her face. She was measuring him up, he could see that, and if she found him lacking, there wasn't a hint of it on her face. The closer he got to her, the more he could smell her. And his wolf could smell her too.

Pulling her into his arms, Graham kissed her with all the passion that was his to give her. His brothers' laughter didn't do anything to cool his need for her, and when he took her hand to find a place for them to be alone, Sloan stepped in front of him. His wolf growled before he could stop it.

"Not yet. There's a problem that needs Ramsey's attention." He wanted to tell her to fuck off. "Graham, calm your wolf please. Her family is here. And I need for them to be put in their place; Ramsey needs to put them in their place. Please, you have to let Ramsey deal with them before I do, and let me tell you, I'd take a great deal of pleasure in tearing them apart right now."

"She's not going to ruin this for you." Sloan nodded and moved out of his way. Graham pulled Ramsey close to his body again and simply held her until she was calm again. Her body was stiff with her anger. "I'll help you in any way that I can, but I think you can handle this."

"I can. I will." But she didn't look ready to handle anything. He could see that whatever her mother had done to her, Ramsey was still hurting from it. "She's a nasty bitch and hates me."

"Fuck her." Ramsey smiled and he did as well. "You're an Emerson now, and Emerson women do not let people walk all over them. You can do this."

Nodding once, she moved with Graham toward the other part of the building to a room at the very back. There wasn't anyone in this room other than the three people standing together, and Graham was sure that was the plan. He had no trouble picking her sister out, of course. But he'd bet if the room were overflowing with people he would have known who she was. She was a simpering, whiny bitch, and she was telling the man to her right about how her daddy had ruined her life. The man standing next to Ramsey's sister looked bored, even slightly embarrassed to be there. There was no ring on his finger, so Graham figured he was Ramsey's brother. The man was a leech. He was also stoned out of his head, and with the way that he kept wiping his nose, Graham would bet that he was needing more of whatever it was he'd already put there.

The second man Graham was pretty sure he knew. And when he was close enough to get a better look, he remembered not just who he was, but what he'd done to Graham while they were at college together. He nearly laughed when he realized how much fun this was going to be for him too.

"Hello, Mother." The woman turned to look at them, but she obviously had no idea who Ramsey was. "It's Ramsey, Mother. Don't you remember your baby girl?"

"Ramsey. And you were never anything that I wanted. My goodness, the years have not been good to you, have they?" But she continued to stare at her for several seconds longer. "Not that it matters one way or the other, but I did think you were never coming back. I had hoped so, anyway. What has brought you back? The smell of your dad's money? Well, you won't get it. I'm his wife, and you are nothing to any of us."

There were several people, his family, around them when Mrs. Stockholm spoke. And Graham knew that she was embarrassed as well that she had shown herself in front of them. But before she could try to control the damage that she'd done all on her own, Ramsey laughed.

"You always did know how to put me in my place, didn't you, Mother?" Ramsey turned to the younger woman. "Deidra. I can see that married life has taken its toll on you. Not working out as much, I'm guessing, now that you don't have to fit into a tiny little wedding dress any more. And Gregory. Stoned like you usually are, aren't you? You're going to have some trouble getting anything to supply you here, I'm afraid. This little town is clean of that sort of crap."

The hand came out before Graham could react, but he need not have worried. Ramsey caught her mother's hand mid swing and held it tightly between her fingers. As they stared at one another, Graham had the most incredible urge to

137

laugh. He didn't, but he had to cough twice to cover the little that bubbled up. From the look on Krista's face, she hadn't expected her daughter to physically take her on.

"Not again. You will never hit me again and get away with it. I'm not that ignorant child I was before, but a grown woman with my own life." The words were softly spoken, but full of the venom that he knew she was feeling toward her mother. "Try this again and they will be picking your fat ass up off the floor when I'm finished with you."

Her hand was released and Krista was in pain if the way she kept nursing her hand was any indication. But it didn't stop her from speaking, and taking her anger out on Ramsey.

"You think you're so grand, don't you? What are you doing here anyway? I was sure that the staff wouldn't have been welcome on the floor with the rich. And I know for a fact that you don't have a pot to call your own." Her laugher was forced, but Ramsey only smiled, never showing her mother how really pissed off she was. "He's gotten it in his head to cut us off, did he tell you that? That's why I'm here, to get this straightened out with your father. But now that I see you, a great many things that have happened lately are starting to fall into place. You've made him do this to us, haven't you?"

Ramsey didn't bother answering her mother, but turned to him. "Graham, this is my mother, Krista Stockholm. My sister Deidra Mosley and her husband Chad. And my brother Gregory Stockholm. They're not really worth the time to get to know, but you really should have an idea who they are. That way when they end up on the evening news, you can say that you met them once."

Graham felt his family come up behind him when he

smiled at the four of them. Ram was there as well, but was standing apart from them. Graham nodded at Chad. He was going to take a great deal of pleasure reminding the man who he was.

"Chad, how the hell are you? Still fucking the prom queen, I see. Do you still sell the answers to the most important tests? Or are you into bigger things now? Say, robbing a very nice man of his money and cars? No matter how many times you were brought up on charges, I'm doubting that you stopped doing the things that made you the richest. Does the little wife know about the three children you fathered in college? Or the way you fucked with my education when I wouldn't own up, you called it, to being the father of at least two of them?" Chad laughed nervously, but before he could speak, Graham turned to Ramsey. "Chad got me tossed out of college my senior year. Claimed that I was a part of the ring that had stolen the final exams and cheated my way to graduation. Nearly cost me my career, as well as some sleepless nights."

Ramsey grinned at him and he winked at her. This wasn't what he'd planned when he came here, but this was proving to be a great deal more fun. As he tried to remember some of the names of the women that Chad had taken to his bed in college, Deidra turned to her husband and started sobbing.

"Children? You told me that you hated kids. You said that you never wanted them." Graham watched Ram as his daughter turned on her husband. "Tell him that he's lying, Chad darling. Tell him that you have no idea what he's talking about and I'll believe you. It's just a misunderstanding, right? Like the two women that you wanted Daddy to pay off for you. Right?"

139

Chad said nothing, but Graham could see his temper starting to get out of control. If he tried to hurt any of them, even Deidra, one or all of his family would kill him. Women, even one like this one, needed to be cherished no matter what. Graham looked at his future father-in-law.

"Ram, you might want to check to see if any of your valuables have gone missing. He had a chop shop while we were in college as well. Ninety or so cars came up missing his senior year. I'm not sure they ever found them, not that I think they could have, but he made some money on them. Or so he bragged to everyone." Graham was really enjoying himself when Ram laughed.

"Already took care of that, my boy. Before I left them. I'm guessing that's why they're here. The money pot, so to speak, has been emptied for them. In more ways than one. Have no idea how they got here, but there you have it. Have you spent all your money and now you don't know what to do?" Ram laughed again, but became a cold, calculating man in the snap of a finger. "Gregory, I warned you, didn't I? I told you to get help or I was going to cut you off. Now that you and this roundabout are in together, stealing from me and so on, it will be my biggest pleasure to have the attorneys do what I should have done long ago. You'll not get one red cent from me. None of you will. I know what you've been up to since I left. Planned for it actually. And just so you know, none of you will be welcome in Stockholm Manor for the rest of your lives."

"Good riddance to the lot of them, too." They all turned to Krista when she spoke. "Ram honey, I cannot believe this. All this time we thought our son was a good man. I'm glad

140

that you showed him the error of his ways. Now we can get on with our life as it was before. I'm willing to forgive you for embarrassing me in front of my friends, but I can see now that it was a part of your grand plan. Catching them in the act, so to speak, was brilliant. As you usually are. Of course, Deidra will divorce Chad, and that will be a scandal, but we'll get through it. As a family again." Ram pulled Krista's hand off his chest and took a step back from her. "Ram? What is it? Is there more that I don't know about? Oh, I don't think I can take much more."

"You knew from the start what Chad was; you and he were lovers during the entire time he lived at my home." Krista looked at Graham then at Ram as he continued. "And I know that you gave Gregory the keys to the garage and the combination to the safe there. You have been taking a little for you both in the hopes that I would never notice. Well, I did. It took me a while, but I noticed."

Deidra looked at her mother, and Graham wasn't sure what she was thinking. Her face was a plethora of emotions.

"No, that's not right. You can't have slept with my husband again, Mommy. You promised me that it was just that one time. It was just a fling. You said that you'd not do that again. You made me a promise." Deidra turned to her dad, her make-up smeared down her cheeks and her face red with anger. "You. This is all your fault. I just wanted to get married and have a really nice house that I could show off to my friends. But you refused to give us the money to get the house we wanted. I hate you, Daddy. I hate you with all my heart."

"I did buy the house, Deidra. The week before you married.

141

Chad knew about it. I even went as far as taking him through it to see what you might need in the way of appliances." The softly spoken admission had them all standing still and looking at Ram. "But it had to be sold off when your husband gambled it away. It was sell the house or you would have been standing by a coffin instead of an altar. I should have told you then what kind of man you were marrying. I even tried a few times over the week before the wedding. But as usual, you wouldn't listen to me."

"You should have just paid it off. Why do you have to keep making things hard for me? What does it matter how much he gambles? He's happy, and I am happy to be with him. Why did you have to use my house to pay off something he did? Buy it again, Daddy. I want my house. I need that house. I'll not hate you if you get it for me now. I won't even bother you about that much money if you do that. I'll need an allowance, but I'll spend it better. No more dresses that cost more than five thousand dollars. I promise. Buy me the house and I'll forgive you."

When she tried to go to her dad and wrap him in her arms, Ram backed up so quickly that Deidra nearly fell. She stood there staring at him as if she had no idea what was wrong with him. Or why he wasn't giving her everything that she wanted.

It was pathetic, and an embarrassment for them all. Not only that, but when Ramsey took his hand and led him out of the room, Graham leaned against the closed doors and thought about what these people were like. She leaned against him and he held her while the crowd in the rest of the building went about their business, oblivious to the drama that was going on just beyond the doors.

"I want to go and get my camera now. I need to hide behind it for a while." He nodded and watched her go. When someone knocked on the door behind him, Graham moved for Hunter and was surprised to see that Ramsey's family was gone.

"Security led them out back to the other part of the building where no one has to hear them. Christ, that's a fucked up family." Graham nodded at Hunter. "Where is Ramsey? Is she okay?"

"She went to get her camera. I think she finds comfort in it." Hunter nodded. Embarrassed now that it was over, Graham looked at Hunter. "I guess I could have handled that a little better with Chad. But he'd done so much to me in college that I let my mouth get ahead of my brain."

"Maybe, but you handled it. And for her. She can see that." Graham nodded. "There is going to be fall out from this. I'm sure of it. Krista does not strike me as a woman who gives up easily."

"Probably not, but Ramsey can handle her. As will her dad. Those two are a great deal alike. I wonder if either of them know that." Hunter agreed with him and told him that he doubted it. "Chad is the guy that got me into trouble in college. I would like nothing more than to see him fall for his crimes."

"Little brother, I'm sure that he's going to be regretting his decisions made back then for a very long time. Shawn is currently going over some other things that might have his name on them, as well as back child support. The man is in for a long and very bumpy road." Graham smiled. "But this thing with the Andersons. I'm worried about you and it."

"Me too." When Ramsey came into the room again, her camera ready, he looked at Hunter. "If your camera man comes up missing, don't look too hard for her. She and I have some unfinished business to attend to."

~~~

Ramsey knew she was hiding. It was what she did best, in her opinion. And she was reasonably sure that she only started taking pictures so she could have something in front of her at all times. It had served her well over the years, but she was afraid this time she couldn't hide enough.

Capturing people and animals in their natural state was something that she was also good at. Ramsey snapped a picture of Cash flirting shamelessly with Margo, and Margo eating it up. Mable stood by him, her face happy and full of love for the man that had meant so much to her over the last few days. The governor was talking with Luke. Jack, unusually still, was holding onto Luke for dear life. Ramsey wondered if he was trying to talk Luke into running for the senate at the next session. Luke was a good man and would make a great senator.

Ramsey could relate to Jack more than the other women of this pack. Jack was a soul mate, Ramsey thought, perhaps a best friend in another life. The two of them, for the last few days anyway, had been plotting and doing it well. Mostly it was the picnic that was being planned for the summer, but they'd talked about a great many things.

Jarrett and Addie were talking quietly in the corner. Ramsey wondered if either of them knew how much they looked like the perfect couple, both of them beautiful and smart. And it was plain for everyone to see that he loved his mate very much.

Ellis was wearing what she could only describe as being completely suited to him. His tux was beautifully tailored, and the tails and top hat gave him a very savvy look. Dawn held his hand like she was afraid of floating away from him. That was another woman that Ramsey thought the world of.

Lee and Kimber both were standing near the table with the food. Each of them, she was sure, had a hand in the making of it, and watched as people came by to take samples of their treats. Ramsey thought their restaurant was going to be a great success, and she could not wait to dine in it.

Sloan came back into the room and seemed to bring all the attention to her. Not that she wanted it, but it was there all the same. Her life had been tragic, Ramsey had found out, and had only just started to bloom when Cash and Hunter had fallen into her life. Hunter, while he was alpha to his pack, never struck her as a man who was comfortable with his power, but he did know how to use it when it was necessary.

People, patrons she supposed they were called, were walking around looking at the different art media. There were woven items, with pictures of the woman who had done the work on an easel nearby. Pottery items, some thrown on a wheel, others made by a method called slump molding. The jewelry from a local woman outshone some she knew to be sold in a lot of major department stores. Dawn had brought in some of her jellies and jams to fill a place that had been moved to another room. People were eating it as if it were their last meal and they were going to have it all. Ramsey walked to her area and snagged herself some of the homemade bread

145

and jelly.

"If I told you that I have a loaf of that bread and some cheese in a basket outside the door, would you come with me and let me make love to you under the moonlight?" Graham kissed her shoulder before nipping at her ear. "I want to eat you, feast on you, while you scream over and over."

"I have to take pictures of this event." Leaning into him, Ramsey could feel this cock. "You're making it very difficult to concentrate on what I'm supposed to be doing here."

His mouth moved from her shoulder to her throat. Reaching behind her, she cupped him in her hand and felt his moan run down her body. When he started walking them to the front entrance, all she could think about was feeling him inside of her, having him take her hard and fast.

When they were at the front, she handed her camera to Cash. If he said anything to her, she didn't hear him over the roaring in her head. Need for her mate was making it difficult to breathe, much less understand words spoken right now. When they were outside, barely had the door closed when Graham shoved her against the wall and kissed her.

"Come with me."

Nodding, she knew that she'd follow him anywhere. And as they approached the park, dark and closed now that it was nearing midnight, she watched him as he peeled his coat off and then his tie.

"I'm going to shift. You, my dear wife, are going to run. And run fast. Because when I catch you, and I will, I'm going to let him feast on your pussy until you can't move, then I'm going to fuck you."

Kicking off her shoes, she took off running. The thought of

him doing just what he said was making her dizzy with need and her pussy wetter than it had ever been. When she was nearing the swing set, he pounced on her from behind and knocked her to the ground. His low growl had her opening her legs for him.

She came quickly, her body so primed for him that it only took a quick swipe of his tongue to bring her. As he ate at her, Ramsey pulled her dress up over her hips so that she could give him more room, and held onto his fur as he devoured her. Her climaxes were fast, rolling from one to the next as his wolf lapped at her. When he lifted his head, Ramsey watched him as her Graham took back his body.

He stood up then, his naked body glistening in the moonlight, and when he fisted his cock, holding himself while he looked down at her, Ramsey wished she had her camera. He was a god standing there, her god.

"I want you...Christ, do I want you." Nodding, she sat up, moving toward him on her knees until his cock was at her eye level. "You put me in your mouth and I'm going to come. I'm as close as I've ever been to coming with you."

"I want to taste you." He moaned when she licked the dark head with her tongue. "You taste delicious. A meal fit for a queen."

"Take me, Ramsey. Please." She wasn't sure what to do, but as soon as she took him in her mouth, she gagged. The second time he moved past the tight muscles in her throat, she swallowed and heard his ragged cry. "I'm not going to be able to.... Fuck, Ramsey, that feels good."

He fucked her mouth, hard, punching strokes that made her want more. Sliding her hand down her body, her fingers moved through her soaking curls until she touched her clit. The moment she did, she nearly bit down hard on Graham. When his cock was suddenly gone, she was on her knees almost before she could think what he was doing.

His cock filled her. His body slammed against her hard enough that she moved over the ground. When he leaned over her, his fingers sliding in and out of her pussy as his cock was, she joined him, her fingers tangled with his as she screamed out her release. As soon as he sank his teeth into her shoulder, Ramsey came again, this time falling to the earth as her world splintered and blacked out.

When she woke, he was holding her. They were sitting on one of the picnic tables and she was in his arms, a place she decided that she wouldn't mind spending the rest of her days. He looked at her when she said his name.

"I'd like to convert you when this is over. This thing with the murders. I know it's a lot to ask you, but I think you'll be safer as a wolf than you are as a human." Ramsey didn't say anything, but watched his face. He'd looked away before speaking to her, and now she was afraid. "Also, I know that you travel a great deal, and I have no problem with that at all, but I'd like to be able to go with you at times. And you with me when I have to go someplace. It'll be hard, what with both of us in demanding jobs, but I'd like to spend as much time with you as I can."

"I'd like that as well." He nodded, still looking out in the darkened park. "Look at me, Graham. What is it?"

"Godan. He's out there, isn't he?" She told him that she thought perhaps he was. "I thought that I'd be...I don't know, jealous I guess, of him. But I feel better knowing that he's around. He...I want him and the others to be able to come and go as they please, but to be with you when I can't."

"He won't leave me. And he is going to talk to you about something later. His brother, Martin, would like to be your protector." Graham nodded but still didn't look at her. "Graham, if you don't look at me, I'm going to resort to violence here."

"I didn't kill that woman. Nor her husband. I want you to believe that." She told him that she did. "I have...since I found her I've been having nightmares. Horrific dreams that wake me screaming. I can see her still. The bullet hole in her head, the way that her body had been ravaged by the water and animals. Someone had tied her to something heavy, and it had...her leg and arm were missing from the weight of whatever it was. I tried to...it was important for me to find the rest of her, but all I could find was the weight. The rest of her was still gone."

"I'm sorry, Graham. I really...." She thought of something that she'd seen in the paperwork that had been given to her. "What kind of weight did you find?"

"What?"

She asked him again, this time trying to calm herself. "Tell me what it was and where it is."

"It's was a rim off a tire. I only know that it was the thing that had been used because of the rope on it. I.... Where are you going?" Graham sat on the table, naked as the day he'd been born, and his nudity distracted her for a moment. "You keep looking at me like that and they're going to find us here in a few hours."

"He killed her." As she stood there thinking of all the

paperwork on the desk, more and more things fell into place. "Holy Christ, Graham, he killed his own daughter."

CHAPTER 9

Krista stood near the entrance to the hotel she and her daughter were staying at and waited. Ramsey was supposed to come by and see her today, and she didn't want her up in her room. It was bad enough that she had to stay in this half star hotel, but to have to share her room with Deidra was not right at all. But that was all that Ram said he'd pay for, and only until the end of the week. Krista had no idea where the two boys were. And at the moment, she really didn't care.

When her…when Ramsey pulled up in front of the hotel in a limo, Krista saw red. How dare her flaunt her good fortune.

"So your father gave you money, did he? Well, I have news for you, Ramsey, it won't last. Once he figures out how much he needs me, he's going to come running back to me." Ramsey just smiled at her. "If I wasn't sure you'd hit me back, I'd wipe that smirk right off your face."

"And you would be correct. Only there won't be anyone to check me this time. I will knock you on your ass so fast that you will wonder if I only used my hand and not my fist." Ramsey looked at her hand. "I would use my fist, if you're wondering. Oh, and the car belongs to Graham's family. I don't have a car here as yet, and they have graciously let me use it. I know that's not a word that you're familiar with, but it means being nice."

"I loathe you." Ramsey grinned and Krista wasn't sure what to do about it. When she and Ramsey had fought when she lived at home, the thing would run off to her room and hide there for days on end. Now she was talking back and being...well, mean to her. "I need for you to talk to your father. I will not let you run our good name into the ground with this mess you've made. I want you—"

"I've made? How on earth do you figure I've done anything? You're the one that fucked Chad. And you're the one that helped out Gregory with his little problems." Ramsey laughed when she drew back her hand to hit her. "Do it and it will be the last thing you ever do in your entire life."

There were people walking along the sidewalk and they were staring at them. Ramsey, of course, didn't care, but she did. Krista had a reputation to uphold, and fighting on the street wasn't going to help it right now. Krista started to speak again, to tell Ramsey what it was she was going to do, when she looked at her. Really looked at her.

She was the spitting image of her grandmother...Ram's mother, not hers. And when she smirked like she was right now, all Krista could think about was when Mrs. Stockholm would look down at her from her small button nose and tell her that she was trash and always would be.

"Where have you been all these years? Not that I really care, but I spent good money trying to find you, and you were nowhere to be found." Ramsey only stared at her. "When I ask you a question, young lady, you will answer me. I am your mother."

"Something that you seemed to have forgotten when I was a child. Or did you remember but just didn't care? And as for you trying to pull this mother thing on me now, we are both well past that, don't you think?" Krista found herself admiring her. It wasn't something that she'd ever thought she'd do for the child that she'd never wanted. "What is it you want, Krista? I have a full schedule today and you're annoying me."

"I'm Mother, if you please." Ramsey only smiled that smile again. "As I started to tell you before you were rude, I want you to talk to your father. He needs to know that I cannot live on the stipend that he has given me. I can't even get my hair done for the one hundred dollars a day that he is allowing me. And I just don't know what he thinks I'm going to do if he follows through on the rest of this. I have nothing of my own. Tell him you want me to have more."

"Did you know that I've been to tribes that can feed the entire village for that much money? And a single family can make that much work for a year to feed and house their entire family. A whole year on what you spend on getting your hair done. Oh, I forgot what you said; you can't get your hair done on." If there was a point, Krista didn't get it. "No."

"No? No, what?" Krista wanted a chair. Her shoes, lovely as they were, were not made to stand around in on hard sidewalks. "Ramsey, I have a splitting headache. No, what?"

"No, I won't go to Dad and tell him I think you should have more money. If it were me, I'd not give you a fucking dime. But that's me." When she moved toward her and ran her finger through her hair, surely mussing it up, Krista stepped back. "Cut it yourself. I do. When I have time, that is. Usually I let Godan or one of the others take a knife to it when it gets in the way. You should try it. It might save you a few hundred bucks."

"I most certainly will not. What a thing to say to me." Krista looked around to see if anyone else had heard her suggestion, and decided to raise her voice a little louder when no one seemed concerned. "Of all the things to say to me. I have a reputation to uphold. People style themselves like me all the time."

"Well, I guess you're nothing but a leader of sheep. And right now, your reputation is in the crapper." Ramsey looked up and down the street before turning to her again. "What is it you want? Besides me asking Dad to give you more of something that you don't deserve. Which is not ever going to happen."

"Do you have any idea how much I hate you right now? I mean, I've hated you since the doctor told me that I was pregnant with you, but now, since you've turned against me, I cannot even stand to be in the same room with you, much less the same state. I even prayed that you'd not be Ram's child so that I could give you to the other man, but it seems you are his, which adds to how much I despise you both." Krista wasn't happy when Ramsey just smiled at her. "You are nothing to me, Ramsey. You never have been and you never will be. As far as I'm concerned, you could rot in hell for all I care if you lived or died."

"That's quite enough." Krista closed her eyes when Ram spoke from just behind her. Opening them to see Ramsey just standing there, almost gloating, was the final straw. Lunging forward, she grabbed for and missed Ramsey, only to find herself on the ground with someone on her back. Ram knelt down to look her in the face while she struggled to get free.

"I'd like to speak to you, if you don't mind. And being as how you are currently detained, this is as good a time as ever." She started cursing at him and he laughed. "This is my lawyer, Luke Emerson. Well, he's not my lawyer, but has been recommended by…never mind, I'm getting sidetracked. Anyway, since you just admitted, in an open forum, the way that you had numerous affairs during our marriage, the pre-nup you signed is in full swing. I'm divorcing you. As of right now."

"You can't do that to me." Ram only laughed and walked away with Ramsey and Luke at his side. Krista tried to get up, but the man on her back just laughed. "Get off me, you piece of shit. Right now, or I will have you in jail before you can say I'm innocent."

"I'm innocent. And by the way, I'm the sheriff as well. Nice to…well, I do try not to lie. Mrs. Stockholm, it is most assuredly not a pleasure to meet you."

He let her go and she laid there for several seconds. Nothing was going her way, and she wasn't sure when that had started. Standing up, she tried to muster as much of her dignity as she could as people started to give her a wide berth. And as much as she wanted to blame Ramsey, she'd not been around when things started to fall apart.

As she was making her way into the hotel again, Chad and Gregory cornered her. She wanted to avoid them; Krista knew that they wanted answers that she didn't have, but she felt like they were all in this together.

"Did she say she'd do it?" Krista shook her head at Gregory. "What the fuck, Mother? You said that she'd do it. Now what the fuck are we supposed to do? I don't have any money at all, and when that bitch at the bank took my card, I had to leave or be arrested."

"She took your card? Why? Did she tell you a reason or just take it?" He told her what happened. That he'd tried to get an advance on the card to tide them over, and she took it and cut it up in front of him. "He's cut us off, then. And they're taking the cards when we use them because they will no longer honor them. Damn it all to hell."

"Whoa, wait a minute. I thought we had a year to use them. I mean, isn't that what he said?" Krista only glared at Chad. Why he was getting anything was beyond her. "I have plans for my money. And the little shit is going to honor our commitment. I might have to have a little talk with him if he tries to back out now. This is not right. I have to have that money."

"And what commitment is that, you moron? The one you made to our daughter to be faithful to her? Or is it the fact that you fucked me in his bed when he was in the study with your wife?" She could see the anger on his face, and right now, Krista felt she could use a good fight. So long as she was the winner. "We need to figure out a way to get back to the house before he does. If we can get some of the art and other things out and sold off, we might have enough to cover some of our more pressing issues."

"Won't do us any good." Both she and Chad turned to Gregory. "I had one of my buddies try and get in to get some of my shit, and the house is being guarded. I mean, big mother fuckers are walking around the place with guns and shit. I even called up to the gate house to see if the guard would let them in for me, and he told me that I wasn't welcome. What kind of dad just tosses his only son out into the cold?"

Krista knew that Gregory was high again. There was a powdery residue on his chin and his nose was bleeding. And as much as she wanted to relieve his discomfort and get him what he needed to feel better, she knew that it would cost more than she could even get with her jewels she had brought with her. And there hadn't been many of those, as Ram kept them in the safe for her. He'd been taking some of them each time she wore them for a long time, now that she thought about it.

Going up to her room a little while later, she sat on the edge of the bed. Deidra wasn't speaking to her. Not that she could understand her with all the sobbing and nose blowing, but she was her little girl. She'd groomed her in the image she'd wanted her to be. And when she hurt, so did Krista. She asked herself again what had happened to everything.

"He's not going to help us." No answer from her daughter. "And Ramsey isn't going to help either. Had I known back then that she was going to take sides, I would have tried harder to at least like her."

"No, you wouldn't have." Nose blowing nearly made her want to throw up, but Deidra continued. "She's just a mean person who gets everything. I hate her too. All of you, for what you've done to me."

Krista knew that she was hurt, but there was no reason to blame this on her. She was as innocent as her daughter was.

Nothing was their fault, yet they were having to pay the price. Life sometimes sucked very badly.

~~~

Ramsey sat at the table, but she'd long since given up on eating anything. She wasn't hungry and had even stopped pretending that she was eating by moving her food around on her plate. Cash sat down across from her and took her hand in his.

"He won't go to prison for this, honey. You know that, don't you?" Ramsey nodded. "I have it on good authority that you found something that will keep him out, and that daddy of hers in."

"It's not much. I have some of my friends looking into some things, but I'm not sure it will fly." She looked around the big kitchen. "I hate that he's not here."

At the crack of dawn they'd come to get Graham. And when she'd tried to get them to tell him what he'd done now, one of the men had hit her. She thought that Graham was going to kill the guy, and had he not had cuffs on, she was sure that he would have shifted and torn them all up. As it was, one of the bastards had hit him with their gun and he'd fallen like a large tree. They had dragged him out by pulling his legs along behind them.

"Hunter is pissed. Never seen him...I'm telling you, if they try any more shit, they're going to have their hands full of something they ain't looking for." Cash patted her on the hand as he continued. "And that Sloan and the rest of the girls? Darned if they don't scare me a bit too."

"Me too, if you want to know the truth." Ramsey had asked Luke to go with Godan to the service station. It was a

158

long shot, but maybe something would turn up there. Ellis and Lee had gone to the court house to get copies of the wedding license of the Andersons, as well as birth certificates. She had a feeling that little Alison wasn't as young as her dad said she was. Then there was the child. Godan had an idea where he might be, but said that he wanted to look into things first.

"You want to know what I think is happening? I might be a thing or two off, but I have me an idea." She told Cash to tell her. "Well, this Mitchell person, he got himself all worked up because his little girl fell in love with an older man. And when she brought him home to meet Daddy, he threw a fit and killed him."

"And his daughter? Who killed her, do you think?" Cash got up and started to make a cup of tea for the two of them. Ramsey had noticed that about the Emerson men…they never assumed that the woman was the only one that could serve. If they wanted anything from the kitchen or anywhere else in the house, they would go and get it, and most of the time bring you something back too. "Cash, you've done an amazing job raising your boys. I just wanted to tell you that."

He looked at her with such a soulful look that she stood up and hugged him to her. When he sobbed, she felt her heart tear in two for making him cry like this. Holding him, hugging him as tightly as she could, she cried along with him.

"Their momma would have been so proud of them." Nodding, she told him she believed that too. "And all these grandbabies coming in makes me miss her all that much more. I tell you, sometimes, Ramsey, I can't wait to go on up and tell her what I seen. And then someone will come along and plop one of them babies in my lap, and I'm just as happy to be here as I can be."

"You have to hang around a bit longer, Cash. I've not had enough of you just yet. Besides, you're the glue that holds us all together. I've seen it." He asked her what she'd seen as he wiped at his nose with the biggest handkerchief she'd ever seen. "Well, how many houses have you been to just today? I mean, you've been here twice, and I'm betting that you've been to each of your other sons' houses too. Keeping their wives happy and telling them good things to keep their spirits up while they try and work this out for Graham."

"Well, I might be just going to get me some of their treats. Sloan makes the best blueberry scones I done ever did eat. And then I take me one or two over to where Dawn is staying right now. That woman could make a man beg with her jelly smeared all over it. Jack? Well, she's a pistol, that one is. Makes me laugh when she gets her dander up. She can get it going too. Makes me laugh every time. Then I can see me a little of the grandkids too." He blew his nose again. "Of course, there is that little Hannah too. Prettiest little thing. And smart as a whip too. Kimber done good by her, she did. Addie thought... well, she's a little harder to get to understand. She knowing so much and all. I love her too, you know. Just about with all my heart, like the rest of you girls. I tried to get her to tell me what was what, and she said she can't be doing it for us. There had to be proof."

"That's what we're working on." She hoped so anyway.

As they sat there talking about the family, Ramsey thought of something that she wanted to do. It would be hard to do with all of them living their lives and all, but she wanted to get them all together. She asked Cash if he could pull some strings to get them to the house.

"Well, the only thing that will bring them all together like nobody's business is a wedding. You and Graham should get yourself attached, and that'll bring them out of the woodwork. Might even be able to persuade little Mable to bake you up a pretty cake and all if you do that." She told him that Graham had never asked her. "What do you mean, he's not asked you? Well, I'll…I guess I'll have to have a little talk with him. Might even have to take a little trip to the woodshed if he don't come around some. Not asked you, huh? Yeah, it's time for me to do a little work on that boy. Show him the error of his ways, so to speak."

When Cash left her to make his rounds, as he was calling it now, she reached out to Graham. She'd tried to talk to him earlier, but he was with Luke and Shawn and couldn't talk. He told her that he loved her very much and that he was sorry.

Why on earth are you sorry? And so you know, your dad is taking you to the woodshed. He asked her why. *He's under the impression that you should have asked me to marry you by now. I told him that you'd been a little busy with trying not to go to prison for murder.*

That does tend to put a damper on things. He laughed. *I was going to ask you last night, then again this morning, but you were too distracting. I so love waking up with you naked riding my cock. Christ, do you have any idea how much I enjoy eating you? Having you come down my throat while you scream out my name?*

I kinda get that when you fuck me hard like you're trying to make sure I never forget who I belong to. And I know now. You. I love you, Graham. He told her he loved her too. *Now, before we both get too sidetracked with sex, tell me what's going on.*

161

They had my confession. Her entire body froze up. *I mean, it was all written out with all kinds of details that I had no idea about. It was even notarized. All I had to do was sign it and they'd make sure that I didn't get the chair for the two murders. I have no idea why they thought I'd sign it, but they were really pissed when I refused.*

They really want these murders solved. I wonder why? He said he had no idea, but he had read the entire thing to Luke through their link. *So he has the details that they gave you? The exact wording and all?*

Yes. He had me repeat a few of the lines so that he could have it down. Told me that I wasn't to say anything or touch even a glass of water from them. And I wasn't to spit or to take a piss unless I washed down the urinal and flushed several times. Graham laughed. *I told him you'd told me about the same thing.*

They could get your DNA and use it against you. I have a feeling that if you did anything that they could snatch up, your fluids would be all over the bodies and a murder weapon. By the way, Godan took the gun we found to a friend of mine. He's going to see if he can bring up the numbers on it and see where else the gun might have been used. Lucky for us that Max and his son were hunting on the property and kicked it up.

It hadn't happened that way really. They had been hunting, but their guns had been for show. And at Sloan's suggestion, they had taken a couple of humans with them, just to have a few more witnesses to the fact that they weren't evidence hunting should it come up.

Yeah, that is a lucky break. He was quiet for several minutes and she was just pulling the pitcher of tea from the refrigerator when he spoke again. *I have to run something by you. It may sound paranoid being where I am and all, but what if I told you that I didn't think these guys are cops?*

Why do you think that? He didn't answer her, and she went about making her a glass of tea. She had only known him a short time, but she knew him to be the thinker type and not the thinking out loud type.

It's like what they're saying to me is scripted. I mean...I'm not speaking to either of them so they do all the talking, but they say the same thing over and over. Like they had been told this is what it sounds like to be a cop. Mason, the big guy, says 'This'll go better for you, big boy, if you just sign the confession.' He says it just like that every time. And Dickerson, his line is 'Don't you know what they do to pretty boys like you in prison? They eat you for dinner.' If someone interrupts them, they have to start over too. Ramsey tried to think what movie she'd heard the second line from. *Ramsey, tell me I'm nuts and I won't think on it again.*

You remember a movie that came out about four or five years ago? It was about a cop and this guy who was going to portray one on television or something. And he had all these lines that he said. I can't remember the name of it. But that second line, that's where I heard it from. I think you might be right.

Rushing to the office where she'd been working, she looked over the board at the numerous notes that had been hung. She was looking for a name, any name, that would help her. Then she looked at the picture of the service station.

Graham...I think I know who they are. Or at least one of them. He's the person who runs the station that Mitchell owns. If it's not him, it's his twin brother. He asked her if she could call Shawn and let him know. *Oh, I can do you one better. I'm calling in the big boys. It's not nice to pretend to be a cop when you're not. People,*

163

these people, frown on that.

You seem to have a lot of friends in high places. She laughed and told him she did. *Maybe someday you can explain that to me. I'd really like to know.*

I'll introduce you to them sometimes. You'll be suitably impressed.

Picking up the phone, Ramsey let out a long breath. When she dialed the number and then told the operator who she was, the connection took less time than it did for her to get her thoughts in order. But when he laughingly told her that he was at her service, Ramsey sat down.

"I'm getting married, and some asshole is trying to pin a double homicide on him. I need your help." He told her that he'd be there in the morning. Then he asked her where she was. "You remember Clementine Mantle? I'm here with her granddaughter's brother-in-law. Graham Emerson is my soon to be husband."

"I'll be there today."

CHAPTER 10

Sloan was impressed. Not only did Ramsey get things moving in the right direction to save Graham, but she'd done it with style and without her help. That part kind of bothered her a little, but she really liked the woman. And right now the president of the United States, Mr. McLaughlin, was holding her little girl. She could forgive her just about anything, too, when she took several pictures of the two of them together and said she'd send them to her.

"It's a pleasure to hold a little one again. My goodness, makes me realize how much my own kids have grown up." He smiled at Lea when she burped. "Yep, brings back all kinds of good memories."

When Dawn and Jack came into the room, Sloan wished she had a camera too. The two of them were so awestruck that they stood there with their mouths open for a full minute before coming into the room. She'd done the same thing of course, but no one but the president had seen her. The only people they were waiting on now were Kimber and Addie. And of course Addie's grandmother, Clemmie.

Just as she was thinking about calling them again, the three of them came in the doorway. Clemmie, ever so prim and proper, greeted him with a kiss on his cheek, and Addie just grinned at her. Sloan was going to have to figure out a way to get back at the girl. She knew entirely too much for her own peace of mind.

"Jenson, you certainly took your own sweet time getting here. I thought you'd have dropped everything to come and help young Ramsey here. Especially after all she's done for you." Jenson? Sloan looked at Clemmie when she sat down. "His first name, dear. I've called him that since he was no bigger than a mushroom."

"Of course." Sloan looked at Ramsey, who was decidedly bright red. "And what is it you did for the president that will make him drop everything and come to your aide? Details. Now if you don't mind."

"She got me out of a very sticky situation that might have had me divorced before I became the leader of the free world." Jenson cleared his throat before continuing. "Be that as it may, I'm here to help young Graham out and to see about Mitchell once and for all. I have had my eye on him for a while now. Did you know that he's here? Renting a house down on… Maple, I think. Anyway, he's there and I have a team watching his every move. His police are there as well. More than likely reporting to him every move you all make."

"Why Graham? Do you know?"

Dawn looked so nervous to speak to the president that Sloan reached over and put her hand on hers. She was still a little shy around people, and Sloan could only guess what having a man like this in her presence was doing to her. It was

166

even making Sloan giddy.

"I think I do, as a matter of fact." He pulled out some files and handed them all sheets of paper from it. "About five months ago, Graham sat on a committee that was fighting the water pollution of the lakes and waterways around the area. Five of these areas that Graham and his study had targeted were part of companies that Mitchell owns. When Graham won, it set Mitchell's company back millions. And he lost the rights to a great many government contracts that were set to be his."

"And his daughter? Did he kill her just to get Graham in trouble?" Jenson shook his head at Jack. "Thank fucking God. He would have been one cold bastard to have done that just to get back at him."

"His daughter. I knew her. Sweet little thing, and so much in love with Peter. I'm surprised that they waited until she got out of school before they ran off to get married." Sloan frowned. "What is it?"

"The report said that she was only sixteen. And he was about ten years older." Jenson shook his head and rummaged through his file again. "You said she was a little thing. Could that be something that someone used to determine her age?"

"I have no idea. But that's why I sent for her records." Ramsey handed her a copy of what looked like a record of birth and a marriage certificate. "She was eighteen when she married Peter. And twenty six when they came up missing. The birth record that we were given had been doctored. And there's something else."

Sloan looked at the records, the originals and the ones that had been doctored. When Ramsey handed her another sheet of paper after she'd passed on the ones she had, Sloan looked at her.

"No." Ramsey nodded. "There's a child out there somewhere? Do you know where it is? We have to…. What if it's still at their home? Oh God, that poor…. Oh, that poor little boy. He's an orphan now."

Ramsey looked…well, what came to mind was pissed. And the president was looking at her like he was sorry that he knew whatever it was that had her upset. Before she could ask him or her about it, Sloan was handed a picture of the little boy.

"Ramsey had me look into a few things before coming here." She passed the picture on to Jack and waited for what she knew was going to be horrific. "He's been…Christ, how can I say this without it sounding like I've made it up? His grandfather has him at his estate. We think…so far as I can find out from the information that I got before leaving, he's been there about a month, since about the time the first body, his mother, came to be in Graham's waterway. That's not where she was killed, however. If the coroner has it right, she was bludgeoned to death."

"He killed his daughter and took her son." Jenson nodded and sat down. "Do you think he killed them for the boy?"

Sloan hoped that Kimber's question was going to be wrong. That he'd not killed the kid's parents so that Mitchell could take the boy from them. But she had a feeling that he'd done just that.

"I don't think it was his intention to kill them both. Peter for sure. He was making noises about Mitchell and his crappy practices. And it was starting to make the papers. Alison supported Peter, it looks like, but we're not sure just yet." Ramsey sat down as she continued. "His daughter was killed first, we think, and then Peter second. The decomposition on the body tells us that. But it's hard to tell because she'd spent so much time in the water."

"So he killed his daughter for whatever reason. Then the son-in-law to shut him up, takes the boy from the house, and then blames Graham to get back at him for what he reported to the EPA." Ramsey nodded at her and smiled. "You know, you asked me once if we got that smile when we became an Emerson. I think you have it in spades. What is your plan to make this prick pay? Because I'm going to be in on it or I'll never forgive you."

"We're all in on it. The women anyway. The men will... well, it would be better for everyone if we handled it. It will play better in the long run." Sloan looked at Addie, who hadn't said a word since she'd gotten here. But Sloan did remember her telling them once that they'd have to surround Graham like a wagon train under siege. When Addie winked at her, Sloan felt like the weight of the entire thing had been lifted from her heart. Graham was going to be just fine. Or so she hoped.

~~~

Al Mitchell hung up the phone. Christ, the kid was being more of an issue than he'd thought he would be. All someone had to do was to make sure that he wasn't seen for a while, and now it seemed that the kid, a little boy, had his entire household up in arms. He'd finally told the housekeeper to hire a nanny to care for him and make sure she knew what he wanted. No one was to know about him or where he was.

"Sir, there's a call for you. Mr. Luke Emerson. He said that it's important." Al asked if he'd called directly or through his office. "Office, sir. I assure you, no one knows that you're here."

"They'd fucking better not if you want to keep your job." He wondered what the brother of Graham would want with him. To beg for something, no doubt. But as far as the world knew, Al hadn't done a thing to connect him with Graham and his unfortunate problems of late.

"Senator Mitchell, it's Luke Graham. I was calling to see if you'd gotten the email on the grand opening of the restaurant that my sister-in-law is opening. Should be quite a showing for you. A lot of hands to press for money and so on." Al snapped his fingers for his aide to bring him what he had on the Emerson family. He had no idea what Luke was talking about.

"Restaurant, you say? Can't say that I remember seeing it. Let me have a look again." The email had been printed and was handed to him now. "Ah yes, I see. Two weeks from today it says. I'll have to check my calendar, but I don't think there will be any issues. I'll have my aide call and confirm once we go over it. Are there any good hotels in the area?"

"Why yes, there are two. One is very nice, and I'm sure is up to your standards. Also a few houses you could rent." Luke named the one that he was currently staying in. "I understand the views from the upper bedroom floors of the hotel are spectacular in the evening. I haven't been there myself, but you'll have to let me know."

Al felt something stir over his skin. He was almost positive that Luke knew he was here and having fun with him at his

170

expense. But Al had been assured and reassured that no one, not even his secretary, knew where he was.

"I'll let you know if I get around to staying there." The laughter was a little long from Luke, and the finger of fear danced over his skin again. "Where the hell is this Somerville anyway? Sounds like it's off the beaten path."

"Oh, it is. We love it here. My family and I have built homes and have done some major improvements around. You'd like it, I think. Walking the streets at dusk, seeing old friends and new ones."

Al went to the window and looked down at the street to see that it was indeed quaint. "I guess you being mayor doesn't hurt either." He realized what he'd said too late. He tried to think how to cover his mistake when Luke spoke again.

"Yeah, not too bad a gig if you can get it. I love being mayor here. I guess you heard from the governor that I had taken the job." Al said that was it. "He's a good guy too. He and his buddies are trying to get me to run for the state senate next year. I guess I'd be in competition with you if I did that, wouldn't I?"

Al laughed. Surely he was joking. There wasn't any competition as far as his voters were concerned. He'd made sure of that. Instead of answering just an asinine question, he changed the subject back to why he had called in the first place.

"About this restaurant. Is it going to be one of those burger joints? I just don't think that would be my kind of thing." He was sure it was and laughed a little about being able to turn him down for that reason. "I'll have to skip if that's it. Ground meat is all the same, so far as I can see."

"Oh no. I don't even think there's a kid's meal on her menu. Let's see, I have a copy of the first menu here. I know she has caviar on it, as well as the finest French onion soup I've ever eaten. Here it is. Striped bass with red rice and green papaya, with a ginger and red wine sauce. Pan roasted lobster with baby leeks and sunchoke puree. I guess sunchoke is also known as a Jerusalem artichoke. Anyway, pan roasted filet mignon with wild mushrooms, which is my personal favorite, as well as milk chocolate mousse with dark caramel and candied peanuts, covered in a warm malted caramel sauce. Very good." Al was impressed, extremely so. "Kimber is really using her skills as a cordon bleu chef."

"Cordon bleu chef? You didn't mention that." Luke made it sound like it was no big deal that she was that good. "I might have to be there then. Pencil me in, just in the event something else comes up."

"I'll do that right now."

As he spoke to someone by the name of Alan to do that for him, Al thought of all the things he had to do before Graham's trial. It would be a quick one, he had made sure of that. And as soon as it was over and Graham was in prison, Al was going to have all his reports redone so that none of the things he'd pointed out were an issue any longer. Luke came back on the line and told him it was good to talk to him, and Al told him it was a pleasure. As soon as he ended the call, Al made another one.

The president had been avoiding him. For the last two months, every time he called he was told that he was either out of the office or he was unavailable. Before this thing with Graham, he'd be in the middle of his dinner and take the call.

Now it was as if he'd fallen off the face of the earth for as much as he could talk to the man. Al needed to secure those contracts or he was going to be broke.

"I'm sorry, sir, to have you hold. Can you wait just a moment and I'll put you through?" Well of course he'd hold, and told her so. But after about ten minutes of doing nothing but listening to canned music, he knew he'd been had. Putting the phone down, he sat back in his chair and tried to think what he could do now. Pissing the president off wasn't a good thing, but neither was the president fucking with him. Once the contracts were his, he'd do everything within his power to unseat the bastard, and maybe run for the office himself.

"Sir, there's a call from your home. Mrs. Mitchell says that it's urgent."

He rolled his eyes and told his aide that he was unavailable. It worked for the president, it could work for him as well. A few minutes later a note came to him that a nanny had been hired and things were fine.

Al thought about his grandson. He was a beautiful little guy, and looked so much like his mother that it hurt him a little to think that she was gone…and that he was responsible for killing her. Al could care less about Peter — the man had to go anyway — but his little Alison was a hard loss. But he'd finally killed him too, and that was what he'd wanted in the first place.

He'd gone to invite Peter out to dinner, or some other ruse to get him alone. But since Peter wasn't there, Alison told him that not only was he not welcome in their home, but she really wished he'd leave them alone. Al had shoved his way into the house, and that was when he and Alison had gotten into a screaming match.

"I want you to forget this marriage and come home. There is no reason whatsoever for you to be living in squander like this." He looked around the small apartment and admittedly had been impressed, but he turned his nose up at it. "You don't have a pot to piss in, Alison. No money for the nice things you had when you lived at home. And since you left, you've done nothing but struggle to make ends meet."

"We have not. Our bills are paid every month. We have food on our table, and we're happy. Something I never was when I lived with you. I told you when I left that I was done with you, and now that the world knows about how you paid off those EPA men to give you a good rating, I'm thrilled to death. You're a monster."

Al had slapped her. It wasn't the first time that he'd hit her, and as far as he was concerned it wouldn't be the last. But she'd pissed him off royally this time, and when she was down on the floor he'd picked up the first thing he could wrap his hands around and hit her with it. Over and over. Her face, her beautiful face, had been ravaged by the time he got control of himself. He sat on the couch thinking how he was going to get out of this. Then a report about the great Emersons came on the television that was playing quietly in the background, and Al knew just what he was going to do. But it had been the noise, a faint little mewling sound, that had him tensing and lifting the lamp he'd just killed Alison with up over his head.

Parker had been down for a nap, apparently. And when he came into the room rubbing his eyes and looking a little lost, Al felt his heart twist in his chest. There was no doubt whatsoever that this was a child of his daughter's. He was the spitting image of her when she'd been a little thing.

He'd not cried or fussed when he picked him up. Shielding him from the mess that was his mother on the floor, Al took him to the kitchen and sat him in the high chair. Thinking about a mile a minute on what he had to do, he gave him a cookie while pulling out his cell phone.

Getting someone to come and clean up the mess had been easier than he'd thought. The man he used all the time for such things said he could be there within the hour, and would bundle the body up and put it in his truck for no extra charge. While they waited on the job to be finished, he and Parker spent an enjoyable two hours together. Learning his name from the drawings that had been put on the refrigerator, Al thought of what he was going to do to Peter when he saw him. And see him he would.

The monthly calendar on the pin board told him that Peter was out of state and wasn't expected back until next week. That worked out great for his plans, and he called the number that was attached to the calendar. Peter answered on the first ring, more than likely thinking it was his wife.

"I have them both. And if you have any desire to see them again, you'll come to my estate in Ohio and you'll not say a word to anyone. So help me, Peter, if you as much as breathe a word to the public about this, I will kill them both." Peter asked him how he knew he wasn't lying. Al pinched the child hard enough to make him scream, and that was enough to convince him. "Now, you're going to meet me, and alone, or you'll never see them again."

Peter, of course, had agreed. The man had to know that Al was a man of his word. Not much of it good, but he did follow through on things when he needed them to happen. And a week later, much to his surprise, Peter had met him just where he'd told him to.

"Where are they? I want to see my wife and son." Al just laughed and let him see Parker, but at a distance. The woman holding his hand, of course, wasn't Alison, but he would never find that out. "What is it you want? Anything, just don't hurt them."

"Oh, what I want, I have, Peter. And had you done just what I told you to do, then this wouldn't be necessary. Of course, I'd not have that beautiful little boy over there, but that's neither here nor there." Peter asked him again what it was he wanted. "You to be dead. That was my plan all along."

"No." Al nodded and pulled out the gun. "Please. Don't do this. If you'll not do this now, I won't talk about you and your plans again. Please, don't kill me in front of my family. Please, have some heart."

"I have plenty of that to go around." He shot him in the shoulder and laughed. "Does it hurt, Peter, my boy? I'll let you in on a little secret…that's nothing compared to what else I'm going to do to you. And so you know, Alison is dead too. I'm going to raise up your son to be just like me. A crook, as you called me once. But a wealthy one."

Peter sobbed. Sat there on his knees and sobbed. When he looked to where his son was, Al told the girl to take him away. And when she did, Peter looked at Mitchell with tears still staining his face and smiled. That had, more than anything that he'd ever done, scared the shit out of him. But his next words were just as chilling.

"You're going to go down. Maybe not for this or for

killing my wife." He sobbed again but continued. "Maybe not for killing us, but someday, very soon, you're going to be so fucked, and I'm going to be laughing from wherever I am at the fall of the great Al Mitchell."

"You mean from hell." The shot to his head had him staring at him for several seconds. When Peter finally fell forward, the crew that he'd had standing by bundled him up as well and took him to the Emerson property. It was just his good luck that Graham had found both bodies. And now things were starting to fall in his favor.

"Finally."

CHAPTER 11

Ramsey stood holding Graham between the bars the best she could. Two men were standing with them, but they had turned their backs to them as soon as she started crying. Graham kept telling her he loved her over and over, and she told him the same.

"We're going to get you out of here." He said he knew that. "I mean, this shit is no way to live. I need you at my side. In our bed."

"Oh baby, I want to be there too. Christ, I have missed you." She could only stay ten minutes every four hours. Luke was working on getting that restriction taken off, but so far he was being stonewalled at every turn. "I heard that they already set up a trial date. That was certainly fast."

"It's fine. We're ready now." And she was. They all were. "You'll be surprised what sort of things a bunch of women can pull together when they're all in one room." He laughed and pulled her closer. "I'm going to see if I can get you something better to eat. You've lost weight. A lot of it."

"I'm fine now. More than fine to be able to touch you."

179

They were speaking quietly. Luke had told them that there were more than likely cameras and listening devices all over the place. "I can't wait for this to be over. I need to be with you."

"Soon. I promise you, soon." Looking at the two men, Ramsey reached out and ran her fingers over Graham's forehead as she spoke to him through their link. *We have enough evidence to end this now, but Shawn and Luke think a public trial will make things go better for everyone. I have to agree. We've got some pretty damning evidence on who really killed them both.*

I've been thinking about that too. It was Al Mitchell, wasn't it? She should have known that he'd be able to figure it out. *I have a lot of time on my hands and have been thinking of a great many things.*

He killed his daughter and Peter, and then blamed you by planting them in your path. There is a little boy too. Al doesn't know it yet, but we've got someone in his house that at the right moment is going to take him from the house. A team is waiting to put him into protective custody as soon as they get the okay. He told her that was a good idea. *We're afraid if he gets wind of any of this, he'll bolt. We've had someone put a hold on all of his accounts so that he can't run. Also, his house is under constant surveillance so that he can't get to his money that he has stashed there.*

You have been busy. He kissed her again. *Hunter came to see me last night. He was telling me that Al is in town and that Luke traced a call to him. I'm guessing that you have all the Emerson boys helping you. Dad can't come here; he said it's just too hard on him seeing one of his boys like this. But he has talked to me a great deal. He told me that he's been spending time with you.*

He has it in his head that we need a garden. I have no idea why he'd think either of us would have time to work it, but he's got this big tractor over there plowing it up. I swear to you, we could plant enough food in that to take care of a small to medium sized country. Graham laughed, as she'd hoped he would. *I'm on hold for an assignment. When you're out, and after a long time in our bed getting reacquainted, I have to go to South Africa for a shoot. Do you want to come with me?*

I think it will take more than a night or two, but yes, I'd love to go with you. How long are you going to have to be gone? She told him about two months. *Good, that sounds good. I have no idea what to expect, so you'll have to get me gear or whatever you and I will need.*

It was small talk, something that she rarely engaged in. But it was also calming to talk about something that was not related to life right now. After finding out if he had ever camped before, she told him what they would need. The look on his face was priceless.

What? You don't think you can live out of one backpack for two months? It's kinda fun. Or course, there is hardly enough water to drink, much less bathe in. And the food, when you can get it, is usually tasteless and sometimes…well, we won't go into that before you get there. But we will bring some stomach meds for you, just in case.

You're not making this sound like a good trip for me. Are you trying to scare me off? She told him no, she was keeping the really horrible stuff to herself. *Really?*

It's days and nights of endless heat and dust. Bugs and things that you have to be careful of because a bite from some will kill you. We get meat, but not a lot. The smell of it cooking will scare away whatever it is I'm looking to capture. He asked her what she was going for. *There are vultures that live there that are on the endangered list. The Cape vulture. I'm going to see if I can get some pictures and film of them in their natural habitat. It's a lot of climbing, but well worth it when you get to see them. And a cheetah. I've only shot about three of them in all the times I've been there, so I'm hoping that I can get a few pictures of them in a den with their cubs.*

Who's sending you on this assignment? She told him. *I work with them sometimes. When there is a problem that they can't get attention for, I can go in and do some testing for them to see if it's environmental or something else. Usually it's that, and coastal development.*

"Time's up, Mrs. Emerson." Ramsey kissed Graham again and held him for as long as she could. The man that had told her that she had no more time left cleared his throat after a few seconds, as if to remind her.

"I love you, Graham. Just a few more days and this will be over."

He held her hand until they could no longer reach each other, and she left him standing at the bars. As soon as she was out to her car, Ramsey started crying like her heart was being ripped from her chest. And that was exactly how it felt.

The trial was set. The way she and the others were working things, it wasn't going to last that long. Nothing was going to be left to chance. They were as prepared for the events to follow as if they were an army waiting for battle. She supposed in a way that it was. And then there was the package that had been delivered to the newspaper in the town where Peter and Alison had lived.

She'd only seen the letter that had been attached to the

DVD, but it was enough to let her know that it was going to be over a lot sooner than anyone could have guessed. In it, Peter claimed that if someone was reading the letter, then he was dead and his wife and child were still in the clutches of her father. He hadn't known beforehand, apparently, that she was dead and Parker, his son, had been taken. After watching the DVD with the Feds, the president had taken Clemmie aside and talked to her for over two hours before he came to talk to the rest of the family.

"It's a recording of a conversation between Peter and Al. In it, Mitchell tells him how he's taken his son and that he murdered Alison. Then he kills him." Jenson sat down. "I have to go back to the White House for a couple of days to clear some work. Then on Wednesday I'll be back to finish this. When I do, I'll have made plans for the care of the child, as well as Mitchell's capture. Then we'll get Graham released back to his home."

And tomorrow was the big day. She'd have Graham back, his name would be cleared, and a monster would be in jail. But for some reason, Ramsey had a feeling he'd never make it there. It was something that Clemmie had said to her just before going to see Graham today.

"When this is said and done, the only thing you're going to have to worry about is that mother of yours. And if you'll allow me, I'll put her in her place for you." Ramsey asked her if that was what was going to happen or what she wanted to happen. "Don't be a smart ass, young lady. It's what is needed. And when you go to that court thing tomorrow, sit in the back with the rest of the women. Sitting in the front will be dangerous."

"What about Graham? Will he be safe up front with Luke?" Clemmie only patted her on the cheek and told her he was always going to be safe, both of them would. After she thought about it, she wasn't sure if Clemmie meant that she and Graham would be safe or Luke and Graham would be. Either way, she was going to be in the back of the courtroom when things started to happen.

Going back to the house seemed so lonely that Ramsey found herself at the diner. Sitting at the booth in the back, she wasn't surprised to see the other women of Graham's family joining her. They had been like a pack since he'd been put in jail the second time.

"I've been thinking of the menu at the restaurant." Everyone groaned. Kimber had changed her mind about things several times in the last few days. "Well, I want things to be perfect for our grand opening."

"The food is wonderful, the menu is beautiful, even if I do say so myself. And so you know, if you make me taste one more dessert, I'm going to have to be put on bed rest because I won't be able to walk anywhere for being so fat." They all laughed at Jack, who had designed and printed the menu four different times now. "It's perfect. I'm not just saying that either. I cannot wait to see you open so you can see what the rest of us already do. That you're going to be a great success."

"I hope so. But you have no idea how...okay, you probably do know how nervous I am. But I want this to work. For all of us. It's like saying, here we are, world, and we cannot be put down again."

Ramsey had to agree with that. Since meeting this family, things were pretty good. And she was hoping that as soon as she and Graham got back from her work, they'd start a family together.

After enjoying dinner with her friends, Ramsey ended up staying with Hunter and Sloan for the night. Their house was closer, but it was mostly because she didn't want to be at the house alone again. Cash was there, of course, but he was coming in later and later now that he and Mable had announced that they were getting married at Christmas.

Laying on the borrowed bed, she thought of her mother. She'd called her today, telling her that she was going to be at the courthouse to see her husband fail. Krista, as she had begun calling her mother all the time now, had even announced that Deidra and Chad had worked things out and that Gregory was now in rehab.

"Not the place he could have been if your father would just give us the money to pay for it, but it's what your father had insisted on before he left us this way. I have no idea what I'm going to do in that big house without him there all the time, but you'll see, your father will come around and things will be just the way they were before."

"You really think so, do you? And what is it he's going to come around to, Krista? You having affairs with your son-in-law, or the fact that you're nothing but a money hungry bitch that has to be in the limelight all the time or you just can't live with yourself?" Krista's sharp intake of breath was audible over the line. "I haven't shocked you, have I? I would have thought with you being the way you are, nothing would surprise you any longer."

"And what is it that you think I am, Ramsey? And you'll call me mother from now on, or so help me, I'm going to have your father cut you off without a dime. We'll see how well you do on your own." Ramsey just laughed. "You think it's funny now, but it won't be when I get back into power."

"Is that what it is? Power? Not love or companionship?" Krista had snorted. "I see. Well, here's a news flash for you, Krista. I don't want anything that he has. Not his money or his good name. I have that all on my own."

The line had gone dead. Ramsey wasn't sure if her phone had finally been cut off, which her dad had told her was going to happen, or she'd hung up on her. Either way, Ramsey was glad that it had ended. She'd had more than enough of her mother for two lifetimes.

~~~

Graham sat in the darkened cell and thought about his life so far. It had been good the last few years. He had a good job, a nice home, and a soon to be wife. He knew that this thing with Mitchell was going to go his way; there were too many things going against Mitchell for it not to. And Luke had told him about the DVD that Peter had left.

"I guess he figured that something would happen. And had this friend of his go and retrieve it should he come up missing. It had taken him a couple of weeks to get to it, and then it took a week for anyone to open it to see what it was. It's pretty damning all by itself." Graham was sad for the man. To know that he was going to die so young. Lee touched his mind just before he saw a shadow move in front of him.

"I have you something to eat." Lee and Kimber moved forward out of the shadows. "Ramsey said that you're not eating well, and we thought you'd enjoy this."

Kimber disappeared just as he uncovered the dish that

Lee handed him. It was a thick roast beef sandwich and some hot french fries. He was nearly done with it when Lee sat down on the floor.

"So? How you been?" Lee laughed when Graham growled at him. "I have another surprise for you too, but we're going to wait until you're done eating. At this rate, it might be sooner than we thought."

"I'm a man on edge, Lee. Tell me or fuck off." They both laughed as Lee handed him a pie. Not a slice, but an entire cherry pie. "This is wonderful. You have saved me the problem of going to court in the morning looking like a starved man."

He nearly dropped the pie plate when Ramsey moved to stand beside him. Reaching out slowly, just knowing it was a dream, he touched her cheek with his fingers and sobbed. Taking her into his arms, he looked over at his brother and Kimber.

"We'll be back in the morning to get her. Don't scream, and for the love of everything, don't tell anyone what we can do. There will be prisoners all over the world wanting us to sneak in their loved ones." Then they were gone.

Graham might have answered but he wasn't sure. He was more concerned with the woman in front of him.

"Kimber just popped into my room and told me to get dressed. Then she said never mind, there wasn't time. I had no idea she could do that." Graham kissed her, pulling her body flush with his. "I need you. Please, I really need you."

Dropping to his knees in front of her, Graham pulled her panties off and licked her. Christ, if there was anything that tasted better than Ramsey, he wasn't sure he could handle eating it. When she cried out softly that she was coming, he sucked her clit into his mouth and sucked hard until she was rocking her pussy into his mouth. Her juices were running down his chin and he wanted more.

Lifting his head from her, he told her to lay down. The floor was hard, but right now he didn't care if it was covered in needles too, he needed all of her. When she was down and spread out for him, Graham stood up and stripped out of his sweat pants and tee and got back on the floor. He was so hungry for her that he had no idea where to begin.

"Make me come." He slid his fingers into her pussy and watched her face. "Oh yes, that's it. I want to feel you fucking me too. And to taste you when you come down my throat. Oh, Graham, I'm coming."

He feasted on her while she came again. Each time she told him it was enough, it was her turn, and he would double his efforts to have her come again. Finally his body couldn't wait any longer and he moved up her body, biting and tasting her as he went.

Her nipples were his favorite part about her breasts. They were thick, about as thick as his thumb, and he could suckle them all night without ever touching her anywhere else. He was sure if he tried hard enough that he could make her come by just sucking at her nipple, but he needed to be inside of her or he was going to come all over her instead.

Moving to her mouth, he kissed her hungrily. Fisting his cock, guiding it just to her entry, he could almost feel her sheath trying to pull him deep. Sliding just to his crown, Graham moaned when she lifted her hips up to meet his strokes. Cupping her breast in his free hand, he slammed home just as he bit deeply into her throat.

Her scream was loud, muffled some by his hand over her mouth, and he was sure that it was going to bring everyone running. But when nothing happened, he moved in and out of her hard, pounding her hard enough to have her crying out with each thrust. When his balls tightened up around his throat, or so it felt like, he told her to bite him, and when she sank her teeth into his shoulder and tore at his muscles, Graham came so hard that he saw stars just before things sort of dimmed out.

He had no idea how long he'd been out. It wasn't long, he supposed. Ramsey was still with him, and her body was wrapped tightly around his still. Moving again, his cock still stone hard, he watched her face this time, wanting to see her when she came again.

"You're so beautiful when you come. I love the way your eyes go unfocused and your nipples get harder. Christ, you have no idea how much I love you." He fucked her hard, not caring now if anyone heard them. "Come for me, Ramsey. Come again and let me fill you with my seeds."

Her body bowed up off the floor as every part of her seemed to be poised on the edge of something. When she dug her nails into his shoulder and screamed, Graham watched her in awe. Nothing in the world could have been more beautiful to him at that moment. And when she cried out again, her body nearly bucking him off, Graham felt his own release seemingly run up over him and slapping out of him. He felt his release from the bottom of his feet to the top of his head and then back again. Dropping over her, Graham didn't even have the strength to move off her, knowing that he had to be too heavy.

When he felt that he had just enough energy to move without having a stroke, he rolled to his back, taking her with him. His arms were lax at his side and her head was laying on his chest, where he knew that she could hear his pounding heart.

"We'll have to thank them for this." Graham told her she was right. "I mean, really have to work hard on finding them something really special for doing this for us."

"I agree. I didn't even know that she could do this. I mean, I knew that she could move through space pretty fast, but this…this is amazing." Ramsey giggled. "Christ, woman, if you have something funny to say, please do it. I could use a good joke about now."

"I was just thinking about the men on the other side of the door. What do you suppose they'd think if they were to come in here right now? Both of us buck fucking naked, not to mention I think I have cherry pie on my ass."

He lifted his head to look down her body, and sure enough, she had large chunks of crust and cherries all over her ass. Graham reached down and picked a nice sized piece off her bottom and offered it to her. When she declined, he tossed it out of the cell. He had no idea where the rest of it was, but right now, he really didn't care.

"I was thinking of us tonight, right before Kimber came and spirited me away. What are we going to do about our kids?" He asked her what she meant. "Well, we both travel a great deal, right, and sometimes it's not really a good place to have a family, but to be honest with you, I'd really like to try and take our kids with us. I mean, so long as it's safe. And most of the time, other than the animals getting pissy at me, there aren't that many people around to harm them."

"Godan told me that he'd protect you for as long as you lived. Then he told me that any children that we have would be his as well, and that he would protect them that way. He said that he wasn't able to take his own family to safety, but he would ours. You think he expected us to travel with our kids anyway?" She lifted her head from his chest and rested her chin on her fist. "I love you, Ramsey. And any children that we have will never feel anything but the love I have for you and them."

"I love you too." He rolled her to her back and moved inside of her. "You told me once that I had to be in heat for us to have children. Will they automatically be wolf when they're born?"

"No. And while my mother was a human, she gave birth to six boys, and all of us are all wolf." He moved deeper and faster. Her eyes fluttered closed and he kissed her on the mouth. "Come for me. I love watching you come while I fuck you."

He moved in and out of her slowly, watching her for any sign that she was close. When she lifted her legs up and wrapped them around his hips, he cupped her ass and brought her up to meet each of his downward strokes. When she came, her body pulled at his, her sheath milking him until he came too, filling her once more with his body.

Laying with her in his arms, Graham thought of having a child with her. She had told him before she fell asleep that she wanted a dozen. He didn't care so long as they were together. He had so much to be thankful for, and having children with this woman would be the icing on the cake as far as he was concerned. Reluctantly, he woke her when Lee told him they would be there in twenty minutes. After she was dressed again and he had on his pants, he held her until the sun started to fill the room with light.

"I want you to change me. Not until we get back from Africa, but right after. I don't think hunting cheetah will be easy as a wolf." He told her more than likely not. "I never thought of that before. Of my job and how being a wolf would matter."

"We'll play it by ear, how about that?" She nodded and held his hand while he told her his feelings on it. "As much as I would love to run with you, the thought of you not being able to do your job would be depressing for us both."

When Kimber showed up a little while later, she had a bag for Ramsey, clothing that she would wear into the courtroom. She undressed, not caring that she was naked in front of the two of them, and he didn't mind either. They'd had a great night and he would forever be grateful for Kimber and Lee for making it happen.

As he kissed her goodbye, telling her that the loved her, he reached for Lee to thank him again. And asked him what he'd like most in the world.

I'll have to think on that one. Kimber and I were talking about a couple of things for the house, but we'll let you know. Graham knew that it wouldn't be for the house, but told his brother it would be his. Closing the connection so he could grab a short nap, Graham felt better than he ever had.

CHAPTER 12

The courtroom was quiet. It was an open session for the most part, but only a few knew that it was going on. They had kept it quiet for that reason…there was no reason for everyone in the entire town to come and see the show. Ramsey looked around again when the big doors opened, and nearly burst out laughing when her mother and sister strolled in. And of course, they ignored her. When she started to tell them not to sit up front, Clemmie, who was sitting to her right, patted her on the leg.

"They're fine where they are, dear. Let them sit up where the action is going to be." Ramsey started to ask her if they would be hurt, but Clemmie spoke before she could. "They won't be killed, if that is what concerns you. But you would have been had you not done as I asked. As it is, they'll be hurt only a little, and it will end so many things for all of you."

"What's that mean?"

When she only smiled, Ramsey knew she wasn't going to get any more answers. Her dad came in a few minutes later and sat on her left. The entire back of the courtroom was taken up by the Emersons and her father.

As soon as the room was called to order, Graham was brought out of the little room. Hunter had come by just after she'd gotten home and asked for a suit for him, and he'd been grinning like a fool when she'd stumbled around trying to find it. When she told Graham what had happened, he told her that Hunter could smell him on her and he thought it was funny. Ramsey was going to make sure Hunter was paid back for having fun at her expense.

The judge read the charges that were lodged against Graham. Two counts of murder, mutilation of a corpus, as well as several other things. She was only half listening; watching her mother and sister had her full attention. It wasn't until they turned to look at her that she realized they were hoping that Graham was found guilty. And from the looks on their faces, she would bet they had no idea that her dad was there and sitting with her. The look her mother gave her was priceless, and she wished they'd not taken her camera when she'd gotten here today.

Shawn was first chair for Graham. Luke was with his brother, but he'd told her that he was going to keep his mouth shut. Everyone thought it would be hard for him, but he was there only for Graham and not to work as his defense. When Shawn stood up to begin the proceedings, he asked the judge for a moment to set up the screen. While two men were setting that up, Al Mitchell came into the room and sat on the opposite side from Graham.

Ramsey had never met the man, but she knew a great deal about him. He was rich, or so it looked on paper. Jarrett had told her that what he had and what he could get to were two entirely different things. On paper the man was worth millions, but in reality, he was as broke as her clock in her pack. Everything about the man was a lie, including his sorrow at his daughter's death. He's been mopping at his eyes since he'd sat down.

Earlier that morning little Parker Anderson had been removed from his grandda's home, and was right now being examined by a qualified doctor. They didn't think he'd been harmed in any way, but they were covering all bases. And the home that he'd been in had been taken over by the Feds, who had a special interest in the safe and things in his office, and the people who worked there had been arrested as well. It was going down fast for the senator.

The judge had been made aware of some of the things that were going to happen. He had the president, a key witness in the proceedings, in his chambers, just waiting for the right moment to come out. To be honest, Ramsey was afraid of the man getting hurt. But he had insisted that he'd be fine, and was looking forward to taking the man down.

When the screen was ready, Shawn called his first witness. Jenson McLaughlin was sworn in as soon as he was brought from the little room. Ramsey watched Mitchell to see his reaction to having the president in the court room.

The secret service wasn't so secret today. They stood around the room like wall paper. She counted six of them just in the front area, and there were at least that many more in the back of the room. When he was sitting in the chair, he turned and smiled at the room in general. But she had a feeling he was making Mitchell well aware that he wasn't there on his behalf.

Clearing his throat, Jenson started his testimony. "I've known both men, Graham Emerson and Al Mitchell, for some time now. While I'm better acquainted with the older of the two of them, I have to say that I don't care all that much for him." The room laughed. "But to say that I would have believed that either man would have done this crime? Well, I would have said no. I didn't believe that Graham did it, and to kill one's own child? That just didn't even come into my realm of possibilities. But then...but then I received this from a colleague."

The DVD was started, and all you could see was a picture. As it focused in, you could see that it was a family. Alison was holding little Parker, and Peter stood nearby. They were gathered in front of a Christmas tree. Then as the camera moved, disjointed images came to be seen, but nothing that you could really make out until it steadied, and there was Peter.

"If you're seeing this, then I'm dead." He looked away then back at the camera. "That's the first time I've said that aloud. I've been thinking about it since my father-in-law, Albert Mitchell, contacted me concerning my wife and son. He has my boy. But I think...I'm pretty sure that he killed my Alison."

Mitchell started to stand up, but the men on either side of him pushed him back into his chair. Ramsey had no idea that was going to happen, but was glad now that he'd not be able to leave until this was over. She'd not seen the DVD all the way through, but she knew what it was.

"I've been traveling a lot for my job. It's a good job and pays well. Alison and I were so happy, and having Parker was just a blessing that we never thought of. But when I was out on my job, Al called me to tell me that he had them both. He told me that if I wanted to see them again that I was to come to his estate in Ohio. And I was to keep my mouth shut. If I didn't, then he would kill them both." Peter looked away again, and she could see the heartbreak on his face when he looked at the camera again. "I got home a couple of days later. And there was…I have a buddy on the force, and he came over to confirm that there was blood on the carpets and walls. But it had been cleaned. He also told me…told me it was my wife's."

He burst into tears then, sobbing hard at the loss that he knew had happened. For a full five minutes he went on about how much he loved her and his son, and how he wasn't going to be able to save her after all. And when the camera paused it was only for seconds, but Ramsey could tell it had been at least a few hours by the lighting.

"I couldn't chance Nick going with me. But he did help me set up the camera on the property. He said it was something that he was happy to do for me. I think even setting it up, he figured I was a dead man. Especially when he found out who he was setting it up for."

The camera paused again then restarted. "I go to the property at midnight. I've talked to Al about where to meet him, and I've had Nick go out under cover of darkness to set this up for me. I've asked him not to pursue this as yet. Things tend to happen in a way for Al that makes things like this disappear. Like me and my wife. But he will send it for me, to someone that I think can help. At least, I hope so. This is the last time that I'll be able to…. He killed my wife, and I don't want to think that he murdered my son too. It's just too much to think about. But I know that…I know that I'm going to die too."

The next part of the video was of a field. As soon as there was movement the camera brightened a little, and then you could see Peter. After a minute or two, Al walked into the frame as well. The conversation between the two of them was short, and to the point for the most part. When he'd shot Peter the first time the camera even caught him asking him if it hurt, and how he was going to raise his son as his own. And that Alison was dead. But when he'd shot him in the head, then stood over his body and watched him fall, it tore at Ramsey's heart badly, and she had to take the tissue that Clemmie handed her. After a few minutes, six men came to Peter's body and wrapped him up in plastic, and there on the recording, Al told them to take the body to the Emerson land.

"I want to catch that fucking Graham with his pants down. And having this body there will really put the icing on the cake for me. As soon as they find my Alison, they'll put two and two together and I'll have my standing back. Yes, sir, I will."

The video was paused then and it captured the men at work. And the two that were in the courtroom now, posing as police, were the men who had helped in the death and planting of the body of Peter Anderson.

No one moved. Ramsey wanted to go to Graham and take him home, but there seemed to be a tension in the air that weighed her down. As Al stood up, he drew his arm forward, and that was when she saw the gun. Screaming at them what she saw, Ramsey found herself on the floor and a body atop her. The shots that rang out made her scream again.

~~~

Ram tried his best not to think about all the blood that had been pooling under his daughter. He knew that she was going to die, there wasn't any doubt of it, but he still couldn't think past getting her help. The doctors had said she'd need blood for the surgery, and all of them—Ramsey, her mother, and him—had been typed and matched or something like that. Even Gregory had been tested to see if all of them could donate to help save her. That had been four hours ago.

"She's going to be just fine. Just fine."

He didn't even bother speaking to Krista. He'd had more than enough of her in the last few hours. And since Deidra had been in surgery, he'd found that he really did hate Krista.

Ramsey sat down next to him and handed him a cup of something that had steam rolling off it. Earlier he'd gone to the cafeteria for some coffee, but had discovered that both it and the tea that he'd gotten for Ramsey pretty much smelled and tasted the same. Brown water. He'd dumped them both and told her that the machine wasn't working right when he'd gone back up.

"Graham went to a coffee shop and got this for you." He nodded and smelled the fresh aroma of good coffee. "He didn't know if you took black or not, so here you go."

He took the creamer...another cup with fresh cream, not the kind that you'd find in the little plastic cups. Pouring a good amount in the coffee, he sipped what he could only think of as gold. Looking over at the young man who had been sitting with them since he'd been released, he decided that he genuinely liked the man.

199

"You love him, don't you?" Ramsey said that she did, with all her heart. "I'm glad. He's a good man. Better than I ever was to you."

"You weren't that bad." He was hurt that she'd said that, even though it was the truth. "I think you were just blindsided by Mom. She had a way of making me disappear when the mood suited her."

"Yeah, she did at that. Which was about all the time you were around." They both laughed. "The night you left, I took a good look at what I had done, where I was going and how I was acting. I wasn't very happy with myself. I was a shitty father, and I don't deserve what you've given me since I've been here."

"Yes, you do. She hurt us both." Which was true. "To be honest with you, Dad, I've about washed my hands of her. I never think of her as my mother, and haven't for a long time. I wasn't close to Gregory or Deidra at all, so they were more like distant relatives than siblings. And even though we all lived in the same house, I knew from the start that I wasn't...I wasn't a part of the family, and lived my life accordingly. I think that's why it was so easy to leave. There was nothing there holding me to you guys."

"I'm so sorry for that. More than...I'll regret my decisions for the rest of my life. I know that I can't make it up to you, but I want to be a part of yours and Graham's life. And any children that you might have." She laid her head on his shoulder, and he felt the weight of the world lifted from his heart. "You will make me a grandfather, won't you?"

"Yes. Not right away, but soon. Graham is going to go with me when he can on my job. And I'll go with him. When we have children, we're going to take them as well. We decided that we could raise them better if we're all together."

Ram looked at Graham. He and his dad were talking softly to Clemmie. She'd come along with them, and he'd yet to figure out why. He knew that she'd been a part of Ramsey's other life, and that she'd been helping her deal with some of the issues concerning Al Mitchell, but why she was here was her own story, he supposed.

The doctor coming down the hall had him standing up with everyone else. He looked…well, concerned was a good word for it.

"She's in recovery and holding her own." Ram felt light headed, and was helped to the seat by Graham. "I'd like to have a word with you, if you don't mind, sir? In private, if you could."

Ram nodded and moved with him. Clemmie came up to stand next to him, and before he could ask her what she needed, she told him that she was going to be there for moral support. She suggested that Ramsey come with them. Nodding because he wasn't sure what was going on, the four of them entered a smallish room and closed the door. The doctor looked like he wasn't sure.

"Just tell him. He has a right to know it all." The doctor nodded at Clemmie, but didn't say anything. "Young man, I'm not getting any younger waiting on you, and this man has been stressed for years. Tell him."

"Your blood doesn't match that of your daughter, nor your son for that matter." Ram stared at him, trying to figure out what the fuck he was talking about. "We thought that with you being the patient's father that it would be a perfect match. Or the mother's, but her blood is an RH negative, and we won't use that. But yours, your DNA, it's not in your daughter's or your son's...the two oldest children, you're not their father."

"I don't understand." Ram looked at Ramsey. "What does he mean, baby? I'm not your father?"

"Oh, she's your daughter. The only one. The other two are a match in that their mother is the same, but not their fathers. I would say that they were conceived by two separate men. But neither of them are yours. I'm so sorry." The doctor flushed. "You might already know this, but I didn't...I'm thinking now that you had no idea."

"No. They're not my children, you're sure?" He nodded and handed him a paper. Ram had no idea what all the words said, but he did see that he was not a match to either of them. Sitting down this time, he ended up on the floor. "Ramsey, could you please go and get your Graham for me? I think I'm going to pass out."

Tumbling over, he felt the world and the people around him just simply snapping out. Then he hit his head, and was completely out.

When he woke up he was laying on a gurney and there was a cloth on his head. When he moved his hand to remove it so he could see, someone smacked his hand and told him to leave it there and to hush. Clemmie. The woman could do more ordering than most foremen he had working for him. Then he heard the voices.

"I don't give a good rat's ass what you want. Right the fuck now, I'm in charge and you can go straight to hell." He thought it was Graham but wasn't sure. He heard Krista but not what she was saying, then Graham spoke again. "Fuck you lady. I've had a shitty couple of weeks, thanks to you, and right now, I've got the upper hand. So if you think you can move me, you go right ahead and give it your best shot. But I have to tell you, if you touch me, I'm going to shift and tear your throat out."

Ram looked at Clemmie, who was smiling at him. Speaking as softly as he could, he smiled at her too. "How long? How long have I been out, and what is going on?"

"About an hour. Long enough for Graham to call in the troops, so to speak, and to have Ramsey let them know what happened in the other room. She's fit to be tied, that one, and when she gets turned by Graham, you can bet that she's going to be hell on wheels." He nodded. "Krista found out that you know about Gregory and Deidra. She's trying to convince the doctor that he was wrong. He told her that he'd tested it several times and he wasn't. Gregory has come to join her cause. I think there might be bloodshed when they figure out you're awake."

"Let's not tell them right yet." He closed his eyes. "They're not mine. You knew that too, didn't you? How long?"

"Not until this morning. I'd had my suspicions, but wasn't really sure. I've never really had any contact with Krista, and I never thought to check on the other two." She moved the cloth off his face now. "You're a very lucky man, Ram. What are you going to do with all this luck that has been given to you?"

"I'm going to make sure that my daughter is as happy as I can ever make her." Clemmie nodded and looked like she was waiting for more. "I'm going to sell that monstrosity and buy something here, closer to her and Graham. And maybe, if I play my cards right, I can be a part of their lives when I really don't deserve it."

"Good man." She started to move away then stopped. "I don't normally intrude on people's lives, but I will tell you this; Gregory will die today. I know that even if he's not your blood you still loved him. But there is nothing you can do to save him. He's done this…it's all on him."

Ram lay there for a while longer. The voices outside of his little cubical were quiet now and he could think. The trouble was, there was so much to think about that he wasn't sure where to start.

Gregory was going to die. He did love the boy…he'd raised him as his son since he'd been born. But lately, he'd known that he was going down a path that was going to cause him harm. Drugs and his lifestyle were pretty much a foregone conclusion with that.

Deidra was going to be fine. He had a feeling that she was going to land on her feet no matter what happened to her. She wasn't all that bright and very vain, but someone would always want to care for her. So long as they had plenty of money to burn for her to be happy.

Krista. He had no idea what to think about her, and he found that he didn't even care anymore. She'd cheated on him almost from the start of their marriage, and for all he knew, she had from the first. There would be no money for her. With this bit of news, she'd not even get the settlement that he'd been going to give her. She was on her own, and to hell with what she did with her life from now on.

The process was already in place for them to divorce, and

he'd even thought about putting the house on the market. But now...he wasn't sure he could live there at all, not with the memories that had been created and destroyed there.

Then there was Ramsey. She really didn't need him either. For the better part of her life she'd been doing things her way, and had managed to succeed despite having them as her family. He could see now why she'd changed her name. He didn't want to be associated with them either. And after doing a check on the Emersons and Graham, she didn't need his money either. They were a very powerful family all by themselves.

When the curtain moved open, he stared at the man standing there. Cash Emerson was, by all accounts, the kind of man that he would like to have known his entire life.

"I'd like a word or two if you got the time." Ram sat up more in the bed and nodded at him. "I gotta tell you, I'm disappointed in you. You done that girl bad, and you don't deserve her."

"No, I don't. And you're right. I was a shitty father, and I hurt my only child." Cash nodded and sat down. "Cash, do you think she'll want me around now? I mean, I really want to be a part of their lives."

"You do right by me now, and I'll see what I can work out for you." Ram would give the man anything he wanted. "I need a favor from you. Not a big one, and if you say no, then that'll be the end of it. All right?"

"Yes. You ask and I'll do what I can to get it to you." Cash nodded and sat there for several seconds before he got up and pulled a worn out picture from his wallet. It was of a man and woman, with six of the cutest little kids he'd ever seen at their feet.

"My wife and sons. All of them. I needed you to know that before I talk to you. A man's family, they are all he gets in this world. And you might be able to have a second chance at it." Ram nodded and handed him back the picture. "This here is what you're gonna do for *you*. You move here. Buy you a house and spend every waking minute you got left on this here good earth being with that family of yours. And you pray to the Almighty that you and this girl of yours patch things up. If you don't...well, I've a good mind to take you out to my woodshed, and I can tell you right now, there will be some wailing going on. I'm not messing with you."

Cash left him then. His eyes were full of tears that he knew the man was shedding too. And Ram had made a promise to him and himself...he was going to do just what he said.

CHAPTER 13

The wedding was beautiful. There hadn't been a dry eye in the entire town when he got up there to make his love for his wife known to all. And when Ramsey clicked her camera, she knew that for as long as she lived, there would never be a wedding that meant as much to her as the one between Cash and Mable.

"You think this will work?" She nodded to Graham and told him to call them to order. "All right, but if it turns out badly, I'm not going to tell you I told you so."

"Yes you will. And it will be perfect. You just wait and see." He nodded and kissed her as he stood up on the table, put his fingers to his mouth, and let out a whistle that had everyone looking his way.

"Picture time." As his brothers grumbled to him about how they were hungry, he winked at her as if to say that he told her so. His brothers were the best kind of men and would, she knew, do whatever she wanted. And this was something that she wanted more than anything.

The chairs were brought out first. Then when she had

Mable and Cash sitting in them, the boys, as he called them, lined up in order of birth, three to each side of them. Mable fussed about it being a family picture, and Cash told her she was family now. The women, all of them, were next. And when they were where she wanted them, the children, all of them, were seated around Cash and Mable. Cash held little Lea so that she sat on his knee, and Ramsey caught several photos of him playing with the kids while he thought no one was looking.

Earlier this week she'd gone to each of the houses and taken several pictures of the families alone. It had been the hardest to get with Jarrett and Addie, as they were awaiting the arrival of their first child, a little girl who had been orphaned when her parents were killed in a drug raid. And now other than this one, they were all printed and framed. She was going to print the best of the ones she took today, and put it in the center of the picture to give to the wedded couple as a gift from all of them.

Graham came up to help her set things up. She was glad that she'd put the remote to her camera in her pocket. Getting candid shots for the albums she was making for each of them was going to be epic. And the fact that she'd found a treasure trove of old pictures in one of the cases that had come from a storage unit a while back had made things much nicer. Even the picture that she knew that Cash carried in his wallets had been among the neatly filed and marked photos.

"You do know that you're going to make him cry like a baby when he sees this, right?" She nodded and smiled at him. "Ah, I see. You like making him happy, and the tears are a bonus."

"No. I just like your dad a great deal. My dad…he told me what he said to him when he'd been hurt the day that Gregory was killed." Her heart still hurt when she thought of her brother, but thought that was due more to the fact that she didn't grieve his passing as badly as she thought she should have. "Besides, your dad is teaching my dad a few tricks too. Did you see them out there fishing with the kids the other day? I think that if they bring us one more 'catch of the day,' I'm going to brain them all."

When Graham walked away laughing, she thought of Gregory. He'd been freed to come and see his sister the day that she'd been shot. And almost as soon as he'd been tested for his blood, he'd gone out and tried to score some drugs. Little did he know he was trying to buy from an undercover cop, and when he'd run, he'd been shot down when he pulled a gun and fired back at them. Gregory had been killed almost instantly.

Her mother had, of course, acted like she was the only person in the world who had lost a son. Even after five months, she was still acting as if Gregory had been a saint and that the police had shot him for no apparent reason other than he was her son. There was no talking to some people, so she didn't. Not in a very long time.

Deidra wasn't much better. Every time Ramsey saw her name in the paper, making some sort of play on her wounds and how she'd been mistreated by everyone, all she could do was laugh. Her sister had bounced up on her feet quite nicely, it seemed. Deidra had, of course, divorced Chad on the grounds that he'd been sent to jail for back child support and a long list of other things, and had married a man that was nearly as vain as Deidra was. The two of them were well suited to each other, and good riddance to them both.

The picture was ready to be shot, and she stood with Graham while the rest of them stared at the camera. She'd already taken about fifty pictures of them getting ready, and when, as planned, Allen came running just behind the camera, buck naked, she'd gotten just what she wanted. At least she hoped so. The laughter coming from the lot of them had sounded like music to her ears.

Going into the house to get the picture started, the girls, as they were now called, came in right behind her. Sloan sat down on the couch in her office. Ramsey had set it in there just for visitors, and was glad now that she'd put in a couple of chairs to go with it. They were a large group now.

"I've been thinking." Everyone groaned at Jack. "It's not that bad. But it might go over well. Anyway, I was thinking that we have Christmas here. It's a big house, and then after that, we can take turns for each of us to host one of the holidays. Sort of take the pressure off any one of us."

"I think that's a good idea. But I was thinking that this year, we could have it at the restaurant. I've already made arrangements to have it closed down for the week between Christmas and New Year's, and open back up on New Year's Eve for the booking I have." Kimber smiled hugely at them all. "We're already showing a great profit for the entire year. I'm so excited."

Everyone congratulated her, and Ramsey went to the frame that she'd had especially made for today. As she was laying the picture in with the rest of them, she asked Addie to hand out the bags that she and Graham had set up last night.

"Just don't show anyone until Cash and Mable open this one." Graham and her picture was in their living room, but not hung just yet. As the others opened them, each of them stared at them as if they were upset. "I'm sorry. I thought you'd like them. I don't know what I was—"

"Are you fucking kidding me?" Everyone looked at Sloan when she stood up and hugged her. "I can't think of.... Ramsey, this is.... Believe it or not, I'm speechless. It's perfect."

The pictures that she'd been given had come with a file for each of the boys. She wasn't sure what their mother had been thinking of doing with the files as the children got older, but Cash, in his own way, had added things to them over the years. She'd found a baby picture of each of the boys, and had put them with a picture of them with their families in a large frame. There was a space on each collage to put a baby picture of the wives that she wasn't able to find a picture for. There were only two, and she thought if they didn't have them, their own child would do nicely.

After several hugs, she and the girls returned to the party.

Life, as far as she was concerned, was going along very nicely.

Before You Go...

HELP AN AUTHOR
write a review
THANK YOU!

Share your voice and help guide other readers to these wonderful books. Even if it's only a line or two your reviews help readers discover the author's books so they can continue creating stories that you'll love. Login to your favorite retailer and leave a review. Thank you.

AWARD WINNING, BESTSELLING AUTHOR

Kathi Barton, author of the bestselling series Force of Nature, lives in Nashport, Ohio with her husband, Paul. In addition to writing full time Kathi likes to spend time with her eight grandkids, three children and three children-in-laws. She writes to relax and have fun.

Her muse, a cross between Jimmy Stewart and Hugh Jackman, brings them to life for her readers in a way that has them coming back time and again for more. Her favorite genre is paranormal romance with a great deal of spice. You can visit Kathi online and drop her an email if you'd like. She loves hearing from her fans. aaronskiss@gmail. com.

Follow Kathi on her blog: http://kathisbartonauthor. blogspot.com/

www.ingramcontent.com/pod-product-compliance
Lightning Source LLC
Chambersburg PA
CBHW032121170626
46808CB00006B/2054